TEASE

(a *Take It Off* novel)

You can look, but you can't touch…

Harlow McAlister is a broke college student. When her tuition assistance is taken away, she is faced with a choice: admit to her mother she couldn't hack it on her own or make a lot of money fast.
So she gets a good-paying job.

As a stripper.

She thought it would be easy, but it turns out being sexy is a lot harder than she imagined. When a few mishaps work in her favor, she manages to hang on to her job and catch the eye of the Mad Hatter's best-looking bartender, Cam.

She's also caught the eye of someone who wants to do more than look, someone who's decided she's nothing but a tease.

As the clothes come off, Harlow finds herself caught between lust and murder. The only thing she knows for sure is that her new risqué job is a lot more than she bargained for.

TEASE

Take It Off Series

CAMBRIA HEBERT

Published by: Cambria Hebert

http://www.cambriahebert.com

Interior design and typesetting by Sharon Kay
Cover design by MAE I DESIGN
Edited by Cassie McCown
Copyright 2013 by Cambria Hebert

Paperback ISBN: 978-1-938857-26-3
eBook ISBN: 978-1-938857-27-0

Other books by Cambria Hebert

Heven and Hell Series
Before
Masquerade
Between
Charade
Bewitched
Tirade
Beneath
Renegade
Heven & Hell Anthology

Death Escorts
Recalled
Charmed

Take It Off series
Torch

DEDICATION

I'd like to dedicate this book to my author buddies, Amber Garza and Cameo Renae (Yes, I'm dedicating my stripper book to two women). Thank you for always being there to cheer me on, to check in with me, and for always having something positive to say. Someday we are all going to be in the same place at the same time and I guarantee that it will be more fun (and definitely less embarrassing) than stripping.

TEASE

1

I cheated on my boyfriend. Before you go thinking what a dirty ho I am, let me just tell you, he deserved it.

I mean, I dated a guy for four years, throughout my entire high school career, and I thought I knew him. But then I started to notice the looks in the halls, the smirks from the girls who were supposed to be my friends. And the other guys? They started murmuring the word *ice* whenever I walked by.

Turns out my boyfriend of the year was really the moron of the century.

The whispers in the hall, the rumors floating around? He started it all. He's the one who told everyone that I wouldn't put out, that I was nothing but a tease. He tried to make a mockery out of me.

That's right. I said he *tried*.

A person can only make a mockery out of someone if they allow it.

I wasn't about to allow it.

So I cheated on him.

Shot his "she's a tease" rumor all to hell. That's the thing about a rumor… it can turn on you in three seconds flat. And so he became the guy who didn't know how to satisfy a woman; he became the one who didn't know how to close the deal.

Was it true?

Nope.

I didn't actually have sex with the other guy. I haven't actually had sex with anyone. But a hundred bucks and a six-pack of beer is all it took for the football team captain to say he slept with me.

He got to be the guy who closed the deal, and I got to graduate without the label of being a tease.

So it was pretty ironic that three years later I was pretty much labeling myself with the exact name I tried to get away from.

Except this time I was going to get paid.

I never really thought I would be the kind of girl who would do something just for money. But then I started thinking about that, about what kind of girl would do things for money. You know the conclusion I came to? A girl who liked to eat. A girl who liked to make rent on her apartment. A girl who would never admit, not in a million years, that her mother was right.

I repeated those things over and over in my head as I climbed out of my used Toyota Corolla and stood staring at the entrance to the place I was supposed to be interviewing for a job.

I never thought life would bring me here. I never thought I would've picked up the phone and called this place to see if there were openings. When the person on the other end of the line told me that yes, there were openings and asked me to come in for an interview, I was shocked when I heard myself agree.

But like I said, I liked to eat.

"Just go in. Check it out. If it turns out to be really awful, you can leave," I muttered to myself as I headed through the parking lot, which was surprisingly well lit. The outside wasn't as seedy as I thought it was going to be either. Maybe it wouldn't be so bad after all. Of course, that thought wasn't exactly comforting. Part of me hoped the place was skeevy. Part of me thought that the minute I stepped out of my car, I would be so offended with what I saw that I would drive away toward a safer... more clothing required kind of future.

But I wasn't offended.

And it appeared I was going to go inside.

Before reaching for the door, I stopped and looked up at the giant sign standing tall in the parking lot. It sported a large top hat with a pink bowtie around its center. The hat was tipped on its side and a pair of very long, shapely legs were coming out of the bottom.

The Mad Hatter was a "gentleman's club."

AKA: a strip joint.

And I was here to interview to be their newest stripper.

Desperate times called for desperate measures. I tore my gaze away from the sign and put my hand on the door. As I did, it swung open and a huge wall of a man stepped outside. He had skin the color of midnight, with arms the size of my thighs. His head was completely bald and he wore a black T-shirt that looked like it was going to burst at the seams because it was stretched so thinly across his massive chest.

Automatically I took a step back.

He smiled and it almost ruined the intimidating effect he had over me. Almost.

"Sugar, I think you're in the wrong place," he drawled, a thick southern accent lacing his tone.

Did he just call me sugar?

"I'm here for an interview," I said, lifting my chin.

He grinned, flashing very white teeth. "Well, you definitely have a look that will drive 'em crazy."

I looked down at my cotton floral sundress with little cap sleeves. Was he being a smartass? I hadn't exactly known what to wear to a job interview where the job required getting naked.

"You gonna let me in or what?" I said, crossing my arms over my chest and glaring at him.

He threw back his head and laughed. Then he stuck out his humungous hand. "My name's Tyrese. You can call me Ty. I'm the bouncer here at the club."

I slid my hand into his. "Harlow."

"Miss Harlow," he drawled, pulling the door open wide, motioning for me to enter. "Welcome to the Mad Hatter."

*　*　*

The place was actually pretty nice. For a strip club. Excuse me, for a *Gentleman's Club*, as was so proudly displayed on a sign beside the bar. The bar ran along the entire back of the establishment, with large mirrors against the wall where the alcohol sat on glass shelves and bartenders worked behind a chest-high wooden bar with many armless black leather stools slid up to it for seating. Every seat at the bar was taken except for the very last two on the end.

I wasn't sure what I was supposed to do. I was a little out of my element.

Okay, *a lot* out of my element.

Of course the first rule when trying to blend in is not to stick out. So I spun away from the bar, catching a quick glimpse of myself in the mirrors behind the bar as I turned, and suppressed the urge to shudder. Or laugh.

Ty was right. I did look lost.

The first thing I did was stop staring at myself in the mirror and turn, facing outward into the club. My eyes narrowed a bit, hoping to erase that doe-eyed innocent look and replace it with a more flinty, edgy expression.

I had no idea what flinty meant. But it sounded like I should look that way.

However, when my brain actually processed what I was facing—what I was seeing—and I forgot to be flinty.

The club was the shape of a giant square, with the bar making up one of the sides. In front of the bar, the floor was filled with round tables of various sizes. Some fit two people, some five. All of them had long pastel-pink table cloths that draped to the floor. Around the bottom of each tablecloth was a black ribbon with a giant black bow.

The chairs were all black leather and in the center of each table was a black top hat with what looked like beverage menus sticking out of the top.

The floors were all hardwood. Since it was fairly dark in here I couldn't be sure, but if I had to guess, I would say the floors had seen better days but still had a high gloss so I figured it was being waxed or cleaned.

The walls were all black but were lit up with bright-pink neon signs in the shape of curvy women, top hats, and martini glasses. From the ceiling, lights hung that looked like giant orbs of low light, kind of like there were a million moons shining in the sky.

But the lights, the tables, and the neon signs weren't what the people in here came for.

No.

They were here for what was on stage.

The stage sat directly across from the bar and ran the entire length of the building. It was currently dark and empty, with wide black curtains hanging on each side. A part of the stage jutted out between the tables like a runway, and I could see the rope lights lining the edges, but they were dark as well.

A waitress walked by and my mouth about fell open. She wore black shorts that were smaller than most of my underwear, black fishnet stockings, black stiletto heels, and no shirt.

Okay, she was wearing a shirt. But, really, I don't know why she bothered. It covered nothing.

It was basically a pastel-pink string bikini top— no, scratch that—it was a pair of nipple pasties on strings.

She had really long, straight bleach-blond hair pulled up in a super-high ponytail and a black bowtie around her neck. As she moved, the light reflected off the shimmering body powder she had applied liberally to all her exposed upper body.

She moved through the crowd with a tray, handing out drinks, smiling, flirting, and leaning down over men suggestively.

Were they going to want me to do that?

No, Harlow. They're going to ask you to wear less.

If that thought wasn't enough to scare the flowers off my sundress, the music playing over the sound system cut off and people began to cat call and cheer. Then a new song began to play. One that didn't have words. It was one of those sexy songs that accompanied people jumping out of cakes on TV shows.

There was some movement on the darkened stage, and I watched, wondering what was going to happen next. As the music played, a blue-ish toned spotlight came on over the center of the stage.

The crowd fell silent for one long moment.

She was standing in the center of the light, framed in electric blue. Her back was turned, one of her legs was up on a chair, and a hand was on her hip. She wore what looked like a strapless one-piece bathing suit in black. Long hair was wound up and secured in a clip at the top of her head.

The music grew louder and she began to move. First reaching up with slow, deliberate movements and pulling the clip out of her hair. Blond curls cascaded down her back, concealing some of her body.

The men all cheered.

Then she tilted her head back, looking up toward the ceiling, and ran her hands roughly through the long strands. With a jerk of her hips, she turned to the side, placing both hands on her foot propped up on the chair, and she caressed her leg all the way up to the juncture of her thighs. Her very ample chest heaved with her deep breaths, straining against the outfit that contained them.

The beat to the music deepened and she shoved the chair away with her foot, sending it flying over into the darkened space, and she turned to finally face the crowd.

Placing both her hands over her breasts, she squeezed them, then ran her fingers down the curves of her body. She started moving then, squatting, rolling her hips forward and back, bending over to touch her toes while pointing her ass to the eager and drooling men. She worked the stage like she owned it. Like she was the last woman on the planet and she had enough goods to go around for every man that came a calling.

And then she reached for the zipper on her top.

She slid it down, revealing a little more skin with every little tug. She pretended like she would pull it open and then she would drop her hands, which created quite the frenzy near the stage.

I watched as she lowered it, lower, lower, lower, until the garment slid off her arms completely and she was totally exposed. Now she was just down to her undies and high heels.

Then she started touching herself.

They want me to do that?

There was no way in hell.

I spun around, ready to race out of there like a bat out of hell, but someone was blocking my path.

"Are you Harlow McAlister?"

It was a man in a business suit with a handful of papers. He had very short dark hair, a shaven jaw, and a tan.

"Yes."

"I'm Adam Greene. We spoke earlier on the phone."

"Yes, of course. You're the owner of this place."

"And you're here for the job interview." As he spoke, he looked me over, starting at my toes, sweeping up my legs, my chest, and settling on the top of my head.

"I think I made a mistake," I said quickly. "I'm sorry to have wasted your time."

I started to run. Literally run away from the topless girls and drunk men.

"Whoa, wait a minute," Adam said, grabbing me by the arm and pulling me back into his side. "I'll buy you a drink."

"I'm driving home after this."

"Okay, I'll drink. You can watch."

"With smooth lines like that, you must be on your way to wife number three," I blurted out, then slapped my hand over my lips. *Oh my God! Did I just insult him?*

He threw back his head and laughed. Then he slung an arm around my shoulders and led me to the final barstools. "Actually, I'm on wife number four."

If I were him, I wouldn't have willingly admitted that out loud.

"So, Harlow. Why do you want to be a stripper?"

"Well, it's my lifelong dream," I said, pressing a hand to my chest and batting my eyes.

"Uh-huh," he said as the bartender set a drink in front of him. He picked it up and took a sip, studying me over the rim of the glass.

I sighed. "I need the money."

He nodded. "Do you have experience?"

"Well, no. But I undress myself every day, and that seems to be the most important thing I need to know."

He laughed again. "I like you."

That probably wasn't a good thing.

"Tell you what. You come in tomorrow night at seven. I'll give you a trial run. If you can take it off like a pro, then the job is yours."

"How much is the pay?" I asked.

"That depends."

"On?"

"You and how good you work the crowd."

Work the crowd?

"See you at seven tomorrow night," Adam said, stood up, downed the entire contents of his glass, and then walked away.

Did I just get hired as a stripper?

Oh my God, I just got a job as a stripper. Well, assuming anyone wanted to see me half naked.

Speaking of, I turned and looked over my shoulder. The blond was still gyrating herself all over the place, now wearing nothing but a G-string. I'm sorry, but how did that not hurt? I mean, really, it was practically flossing her butt.

I spun back around and put my head in my hands. I felt the heavy thud of something in front of me, so I looked up.

It was a shot glass. I watched as the bartender filled it with vodka. "You look like you could use this."

I looked up, a little higher than the glass, and caught a set of bronzed rock-solid abs. My eyes lingered and then traveled upward, past the rippling muscles, the smooth, defined chest, past the black bowtie around his neck to finally land on his face.

I understood now why his body was so mouthwatering.

A face like that could only be attached to near perfection. Square, smooth jawline, prominent nose and cheekbones, full lips, olive-toned, sun-kissed skin, and eyes that looked like melted chocolate. I couldn't tell what color hair he had because he wore a black fedora that was slightly tilted to one side, giving him a devilish air.

If he were an all-you-can-eat buffet, I'd unbutton the top of my jeans and dig in.

I stared at him dumbly, my brain refusing to form a cohesive thought, so I knew speaking wasn't going to happen.

He smiled, placing his hands palm down on the bar and leaning over the top slightly, bringing his manly goodness a little closer. "Bottoms up."

"I'm not drinking tonight," I said, proud that I found my voice.

His dark eyes swept over my face and he smiled. Then, still watching me, he picked up the shot glass and emptied it all into his mouth in one great gulp. He set it back down in front of me. "Most girls would have just taken the shot."

"I'm not most girls."

He leaned both elbows on the bar and stared at me. "So I see."

A little shiver raced up my spine. It was one of those shivers that felt so delicious I just wanted to have another. The sound of his voice was like the roar of a lion, the growl of an alpha, because it churned up some primal instinct in me to obey his every command.

Man, this place was starting to make me crazy. I had to get out of here.

"Thanks for the drink," I said, spinning the stool around and getting ready to hop off.

"So you're the new dancer?"

I glanced over my shoulder, looking around the curtain of my chestnut-colored hair. "That depends."

"On?"

"On whether or not I have the guts to show up tomorrow night."

A slow smile curved his lips. "Well, I sure hope you do."

"Why is that?"

"Because I definitely wouldn't mind seeing more of you."

The bottom dropped out of my stomach and I'm pretty sure my cheeks turned bright pink. He chuckled, the low sound carrying over every other sound in the place and echoing through the deepest parts of my mind.

Then he picked up the empty shot glass and turned around. "See ya around," he said, tossing the words over his broad shoulder.

It wasn't until I was outside fumbling around with my car keys that I wondered if he meant he actually wanted to see *me* again… or just the parts of me I dared to bare.

2

I talked myself out of going that night at least a hundred times. But then I would look at the bills piled on my counter, the dwindling supplies in my fridge and pantry and ask myself how bad could it really be?

It was only skin.

Skin that a lot of strangers' eyes would be ogling.

I couldn't do it.

I glanced at my cell phone lying on my bed. I could call her, tell her that I needed money. She would tell me to come home, to get a job at the local diner or the bank. And then I would haul my suitcases into my old bedroom and start my life over again as the girl who tried to get away but in the end couldn't hack it.

Or…

I could pick out an outfit, go to work, and pretend that everyone else was in their undies instead of me.

I definitely wouldn't mind seeing more of you.

It wasn't the first time today I heard that line in the back of my head. Yeah, okay, it probably was just that. A line. But damn if it wasn't working.

I looked at myself in the mirror. I knew I was an attractive woman, with long legs, a thin but curvy frame, long, deep-brown hair, and blue eyes. I looked exactly like the girl next door. In fact, I *was* the girl next door. Until I graduated high school determined to bust out of the small town I was stranded in.

I wasn't going back there.

I was no longer the girl next door.

I was a woman.

I was in charge of my life and my body.

And I was also going to be a stripper.

I turned to the side to study the profile of my body. My boobs certainly weren't huge (not like that stripper I saw on stage last night), but they were a decent size, and they were perky. I had a little bit of a booty as well, so I guess I could consider myself well equipped for the job.

Now all I needed was something to wear.

What did one wear when they were going to be taking it all off?

Something sexy, the voice in my head whispered.

I pulled open my closet and studied the contents. I had the clothes of a college student who happened to live in Myrtle Beach, South Carolina. That wardrobe consisted of jeans, T-shirts, blouses, and beach wear. It did not consist of lingerie, push-up bras, and thongs.

I glanced at the sundresses that hung in a row and laughed.

After the reaction I got to the one I wore last night, I doubted showing up to work in another one would go over very well. Adam would probably kick me out before I even opened my mouth.

I considered taking a pair of scissors to a shirt to make it midriff baring and to a skirt to make it sinfully short, but that seemed like a waste of perfectly nice clothes.

In the end, I yanked out my choice and threw it on, then went to do my hair, makeup, and smooth on some body lotion. My stomach growled during my primping, but I ignored it. I was so nervous about what I was about to do that I hadn't eaten a thing all day. And I wasn't going to. The last thing I wanted to do was get up on stage and show everyone exactly what I had for lunch that day.

If I even made it onto the stage.

What the hell was I supposed to do once I was there?

Gyrate like that girl last night? No. Thank you. But I knew I had to do something. I mean, just standing there would get me fired.

I decided to just stop thinking about it altogether. I was making myself more nervous than I really needed to be, and if I kept it up, I wouldn't go at all.

After I was ready, I stared at the clock until six and then locked up my apartment and drove to the Mad Hatter.

Just my luck, the place was packed.

I parked in the very back of the lot and sat there for a few minutes, feeling nervous sweat drip down my back. Before I could talk myself into peeling rubber out of the lot, I climbed out of the car and made my way to the entrance.

The door swung open and the bouncer from last night opened the door.

"Hey, Ty," I said, giving him a smile.

"Miss Harlow, you came back."

"You didn't think I'd get the job?"

"Nah, girl, I knew you would get the job. I just wasn't sure if you wanted it."

Well, neither was I, but I didn't say it out loud.

"Got any advice for me, Ty? I'm sure as the bouncer you know all the inside information and tricks."

He grinned and regarded me with pursed lips. "Don't be trashy."

"Well, that might be hard considering I'm about to shake what my momma gave me."

He threw back his head and laughed. "I've seen a lot of girls come through here. Some of them are good and some of them aren't. The ones who do the best are the ones who realize there is a fine line between sexy and sleazy. Catch my drift?"

I nodded slowly. "I think so. Kind of a less-is-more approach?"

"There you go," he said, inclining his head. Then he held the door wide and stepped back. "Good luck."

"Thanks," I said and stepped inside.

The entire place was full. People standing around the bar, filling up the tables, and talking over the music. There was already a girl on stage. The pole that stood in the center was spotlighted in hot pink, and I watched as she wrapped her toned legs around it and then draped her body upside down. Her dark hair fell in a cascade and was so long it actually brushed the ground.

As I watched, she moved fluidly, sensually, sliding down the pole and then touching her body in a way that made everyone think touching her would be the most exciting moment of their entire life.

I averted my eyes because I was slightly embarrassed to be watching her turn people on.

"So you showed up," called a voice from behind the bar.

He wasn't wearing a shirt, again.

And the hat he wore last night wasn't on his head. He had blond hair. Very blond and so very messy that it looked like he spent time running his fingers through it all day long.

"Here I am," I said, stepping a little closer to the bar.

"So," he began, giving me a knowing grin. "On a scale from one to ten, how nervous are you?"

"Eleven."

"Oh well, that's better than twenty-five."

"Ha," I said, feeling my stomach do this weird flippy thing every time he smiled.

Adam stepped up beside me. "Come on, we need you backstage."

That flippy feeling in my belly quickly turned to a nauseous rumble as he turned and walked toward the back, expecting me to follow.

"Hey," the hot bartender said.

I glanced over my shoulder.

"Don't screw up."

"Gee, thanks."

He was laughing when I walked away, weaving through the crowded tables and the boisterous laughter.

Backstage was quieter and I found I was able to let out the breath I held. The back room was lined with dressing tables, all with those big mirrors rimmed in lights. There were little velvet stools pushed under each table and makeup and cans of hairspray were scattered everywhere. In the back of the room, there were several racks of what looked like lingerie and a few mannequin heads lining a shelf that had various wigs in every style and color. High heels scattered the floor and there was a small ladies' room off to the left with the light off.

There were several girls back here, all of them in various states of undress. It was clear no one used the bathroom as a dressing room. Of course when you were stripping down in front of a room full of people, I guess doing it in the back was considered sort of private.

"Ladies, this is Harlow," Adam said in a voice that carried through the room. "She's auditioning tonight. Show her the ropes."

All eyes turned to me. I could feel them assessing me, judging me, deciding if they would like me before I even spoke a word. It was like being back in high school where all the girls were catty and cliquish.

I didn't let people push me around in high school, and I wasn't about to start now.

I lifted my chin and went to a dressing table that looked like it was never used. "Can I use this one?"

The girl next to me, a redhead with gigantic boobs, nodded.

I set down my bag and then looked around nervously for something to do. Adam approached; he was wearing a suit with no tie and a pair of sporty-looking dress shoes. In his hand he carried a clipboard that he hadn't even looked at once since we'd been back here.

"You go on at seven. Your routine ends when your song ends. Be sure to tell the DJ what you want him to play."

Oh, shit. I was supposed to have a song?

"After your routine, you can collect your money and then make your way back here. You can walk around in your outfit or change into something from back there." He pointed at the racks of clothes. "Then go to the bar and get a tray. You can serve drinks until your next routine."

My next routine? I swallowed. "How many routines do I do during a shift?"

"For now, one an hour. If you're good, then that will increase."

I didn't even know how long a shift was. I was in way over my head here. Maybe I should just bail now and save myself the embarrassment of getting fired.

I opened my mouth to announce my departure, but Adam cut me off to yell, "Roxie! Get your ass over here!"

The dark-haired girl I'd just watched on stage appeared beside us. "Yeah, boss?"

"Show Harlow the ropes."

Then he left, my eyes following him desperately. I felt like a child who was being dropped off at kindergarten for the very first time. Adam definitely wasn't my parent or even a parental type, but at least when he was telling me what to do I didn't feel so freaked out.

"You've never done this before, have you?" Roxie said. She had purple eyes and hair so dark it was almost black. She wore it sleek and straight and it hung all the way down to her hips. The heavy, straight bangs across her forehead accentuated the odd color of her eyes.

"Never," I said, giving a nervous giggle.

She wore a tiny pair of boy shorts and a glittery corset that pushed her chest up to her neck. Her skin was creamy and pale and she was curvy in all the right places.

"The first time is always the worst. After a while, it'll be like brushing your teeth. You won't even think about it."

I couldn't imagine getting naked in front of a bunch of drunk and slurring idiots would ever get any easier, but I didn't bother to disagree with her.

"Do you wear contacts?" I asked, totally distracted by those purple eyes.

"Yeah." She smiled. "I'm Roxie," she said, holding out her hand.

I shook it. "Harlow."

"You gonna use your real name on stage?"

I hadn't thought about it. I guessed I probably shouldn't. "I don't think so."

"Got a stage name in mind?"

"No. And I don't have a song either."

"Adam never tells any of the new girls they need a song. He's such a man, I swear. He probably doesn't even know music plays around here. All he cares about is making money."

I couldn't really fault him for that. I mean, hello, it's the reason I was here.

"That what you're wearing?" she asked, taking in my skimpy cutoff shorts and white "wife-beater" tank top.

"Yes?"

"Lose the bra."

A protest formed on my tongue. If I lost the bra, then when I took off my shirt, I would be completely bare… I was kind of hoping to delay the inevitable.

"Oh, and Adam probably didn't tell you that we aren't a full nude strip club."

"What does that mean?" I said as she pushed me down onto my stool, picked up a brush and pulled down my ponytail.

"It means we don't take off our bottoms. You can strip all the way down to your panties or thong— whatever you have on—but that's it."

Well, that was the best news I'd heard all day. "And our tops?"

"Yeah, those can come off."

"How long is a shift?" I asked as she teased the hair at my crown.

"Usually the girls stop dancing at two a.m. and then we take turns on who stays to close down the bar."

So that meant I had to do six or seven dances a night. That was a lot of freaking naked time.

She patted my shoulder. "You can do the same routine a couple times so not every time you dance is brand new, just don't do the same one back to back."

"I only brought what I'm wearing."

"Did Adam tell you nothing?"

I shook my head. "Just that I was auditioning."

She shook her head. "I'll talk to him."

"What about that stuff back there?" I motioned to the racks of clothes.

"I wouldn't put that community wear on my body. Who knows where some of these dirty bitches have been?"

My mouth fell open and then we both started laughing.

"It's true," she said with a smile. "Like you haven't been thinking it since you walked in the door."

A little bit of the tension coiling inside me eased. "So how long have you been doing this?"

She shrugged. "A couple years."

"Seriously?"

She lifted one shoulder as she smoothed out my hair. "What can I say? The money's great."

I didn't say anything because I honestly wasn't sure if the money was going to be worth all of this.

"What do you think?" she asked, and I looked in the mirror.

"Wow," I whispered, leaning in. My hair was bumped up in the back and parted to the side so it fell over one eye. It tumbled around my shoulders loosely and flirted with my collarbone.

"You still need something," she mused, then walked across the room to her table and rummaged around in a hot-pink bag. When she found what she wanted, she snapped back up and shimmied over to me.

With a grin, she reached out and clipped something in my hair, adjusting some of the strands around it. Then she stepped back and admired her handiwork in the mirror.

It was a hair extension—a thick strip of purple that popped out against my dark hair and actually played up the blue in my eyes.

I liked it. It was sexy.

"There, that's perfect."

"Don't you need this?" I asked, fingering the ends of my hair.

"Nah, it clashes with my eyes so I don't wear it. Keep it."

"Really? Thank you."

Roxie looked up at the clock and then back at me. "Showtime."

And just like that, my nerves intensified by like three thousand. "I can't do this."

"Yes. You can."

"No. I don't think I can."

"You have a boyfriend?"

I felt my brow wrinkle at the change of topic. "No."

"Probably better that way," she murmured almost to herself. "Well, just imagine there is this really hot guy sitting out there. Imagine you're dying for him to ask you out, but he seems to never notice you. *Make* him notice you."

I nodded.

She laughed. "Whatever you do, don't look like that out there."

She yanked me toward the couple stairs that led up to the curtain behind the stage. One of the girls was just finishing up and the men were all whistling.

"The song," I said, turning around to flee the stage.

"I'll tell Remy what to play. You just concentrate on moving."

I nodded numbly. I couldn't believe I was actually doing this.

"Oh, name! What's your name?" Roxie said before rushing away.

"Violet," I said, reaching up and touching the purple stripe of color in my hair.

She gave me a thumbs-up and then rushed away, leaving me alone behind the curtain.

The other girl moved off the stage and behind the curtain. Her hands were filled with cash. "You're up," she said, looking down and smirking.

It was the kind of smirk that lit a fire in my blood, like she was certain I was going to bomb big time.

I'd show her.

The music cut out. The stage went dark. My heart began to pound.

When the DJ introduced the new girl Violet, I didn't realize he was talking about me until music started playing.

It was Def Leopard.

I stood there, rooted on the stage, gripping the curtain like I was frozen.

Roxie appeared and gave me a little shove.

And just like that, I was center stage, and every man in the room watched for me to get naked.

3

As I stared out into the crowd, I realized something:

It wasn't only men who waited for me to show them the goods, but women too.

Well, this was awkward.

I couldn't imagine why a woman would come here to watch another woman undress. I mean, if she wanted to see boobs, she could look in the mirror.

A spotlight flicked on and circled the room until it landed on me. It was a purple light, casting violet-hued shadows over everything around me. I liked it because I somehow felt it gave me more coverage (hey, I never said my logic wasn't flawed).

Someone in the front row cleared his throat and then the music pressed in on me.

I was supposed to be dancing.

Or something.

I heard some giggling and I turned my head to see a couple of the girls standing behind Roxie, watching me.

I started to move. I pretended like I was a model strutting down a runway, shaking my hips and running my fingers through my hair, giving it a shake and a playful toss. Someone in the back whistled.

I admit, that made me feel good. I looked up to see who it was, but the spotlight blinded me and I stumbled a bit. How could I trip over my own feet? I looked down.

I was wearing flip-flops.

Crap. I meant to change.

Now I understood why some of the girls were laughing.

I stopped at the end of the stage and bent down to touch my toes, making sure my backside was in full view. I'm pretty sure my shorts rose up my crack. It didn't feel good.

But I smiled like I loved it.

Then casually, I pulled my shoes off each foot and tossed them over my shoulder and gave a suggestive little look to the crowd.

That got me a couple more whistles.

The song playing was "Pour Some Sugar On Me," one of Def Leopard's most popular songs. It was a sexy song and it helped me get into the mood.

Maybe this wouldn't be so bad after all.

I turned to strut back toward the front of the stage, thinking I would find a chair and do something with it.

But I tripped over my flip-flop.

I fell right off the stage, halfway across a round table for two.

The table probably would have fallen over except the two men sitting there reached out to steady it.

But I did manage to knock over their beers and a shot, which currently soaked my arms and shirt.

There was some laughter from the crowd, and I was pretty sure I was going to die of embarrassment right there.

"Are you okay?" one of the men at the table asked.

"Sorry about that, guys," a new voice swept in. "Here's a pitcher on the house for the trouble."

I looked up from my position sprawled across the table.

Of course.

It was the hottie bartender.

Because I needed even more humiliation right now.

Our eyes locked.

He winked.

Inspiration overcame me.

"Thanks for the catch, boys," I said in my best throaty voice. I climbed up onto the table, planting my bare feet right there in the puddles of beer. Then on instinct, I reached down, dipped two of my fingers into their new pitcher, swirled them around, and stood, wrapping my lips around both of those fingers and slowly sliding them out.

The crowd roared.

I did a little shimmy and then glanced at the bartender, who was standing there watching me. He held a tray and on it was a pitcher of water.

I bent, sticking out my butt and thrusting my chest in one of the men's faces, and gripped the handle of the pitcher. Slowly, I stood back up, held it over my head and looked up into the darkened ceiling letting my hair fall away from my face.

Then I poured the water over me.

It was cold, sloshing over my face, down my neck, and into my shirt. When the pitcher was empty, I tossed it back to the bartender and turned away to the two men flanking my sides.

"Can a girl get a little help here?"

The bigger of the two men gripped me around the waist and picked me up, stepping back to the stage and setting me down. I was still soaking wet, the water dripping down my legs, and my shirt was plastered to my chest.

My nipples were hard because the water was cold, and the air-conditioner brushed over my skin, making them even harder.

Feeling bold, I grabbed them, gently squeezing, then pulling away.

I knew my tank was see-through. I knew every person in this place had a clear view of my goods, and I actually still felt decently covered up.

For fun, I reached for the hem of my shirt, slipping it up so it showed off my navel and the flatness of my belly. Then I yanked it back down and walked away, toward the curtain.

The men were all going crazy, yelling, catcalling, telling me to come back. So I stopped, looked over my shoulder, flipping my saturated hair, and then I quickly undid the fastening of my jean shorts and pulled them down just enough to show the lace top of my panties.

Then I yanked them back up and spun, facing the crowd and shaking my finger like they were all very bad.

I stuck the same finger back in my mouth and pulled it out before turning around and walking behind the curtain, completely out of sight.

Roxie was standing there with a towel. Her eyes were wide. "What was that?"

"I'm not really sure," I said, my nerves coming back full force. Had I really just created my own private wet T-shirt contest out there?

"Well, honey, whatever it was, they sure liked it."

I glanced around the corner at the crowd. They were all still whistling and catcalling. Dollar bills crowded the edge of the stage.

"Go get your money," Roxie said.

I walked back out there, and the whistling got louder. I strutted around while I picked up the cash and then gave the guys at the table I almost knocked over a wink before rushing backstage to my dressing table.

One look in the mirror told me my water stunt ruined my makeup and most of my hair.

And my shirt was definitely see-through.

Using the towel Roxie gave me, I squeezed the water out of my hair and wiped off the worst of my makeup. I brought a little with me, so I pulled it out and reapplied quickly. Then I pulled my hair into a high ponytail and hoped the wet ends would dry quickly.

I was still too nervous to count the money I made, so I shoved it all in my bag and then put the bag under my table.

Roxie was by the door, waving me to hurry, so I went after her and we stopped at the end of the bar.

"Just go around and get drink orders. Then come back and tell the bar. Deliver and repeat."

I nodded. I used to waitress, so this at least wasn't completely foreign to me.

Roxie disappeared into the crowd so I took a deep breath and picked up a tray. I felt like I was being stared at so I turned my head. Hottie bartender watched me from the other end of the bar.

I gave him a little wave, grabbed a tray, and started to take orders.

It didn't take long to figure out I wasn't really out here to take drink orders. I was actually out here to give the people something to look at, to flirt with, and to generally keep the customers happy.

I relaxed into that role because at least this was something I could wear a shirt for.

Just when I was starting to get nervous about my next "routine," Adam waved to me from the edge of the crowd. I slipped through and followed him into his office.

He was going to fire me.

I fell like a klutz, spilled beer on paying customers, and didn't even take off my shirt.

I was the worst stripper in the history of strippers.

"What the hell was that out there earlier?" he said, standing beside his desk.

"I'm so sorry, I—"

"You're sorry?" He cut in. "That was brilliant!"

"It was?" I asked, shock lacing my tone.

"Every guy in this place had his eyes glued to your chest."

I didn't know how to respond.

"I think you're exactly what this place needs." He went on.

"What is that, exactly?"

"A mystery, a girl who whips the crowd into a frenzy just to get a peek."

Is that what I did?

"Since you didn't bring anything else to wear, you can just serve the rest of the night. But tomorrow you'll be dancing every hour."

"Tomorrow?"

"You got the job, Violet. Welcome to the Mad Hatter."

"I wasn't expecting this."

"Frankly, neither was I. I thought you were going to bomb miserably."

"Um, thank you?" I said sarcastically.

He flashed me a smile. "Who knew underneath that good girl exterior you were hiding the inner workings of a sexy bitch?"

"I'm pretty sure that could be considered harassment."

"Probably. Now get back to work. Before you leave tonight, you can fill out the forms I need you to sign."

Roxie was waiting outside the office when I left. "Well?" she asked.

"I got the job."

She bounced around on her four-inch heels. "It was the water… men and wet T-shirts… gets 'em every time."

"So you think I should add that to my routine, then?" Wait a minute. I was now thinking about my routine? So I was actually going to do this. Somewhere along the way of being scared silly and shaking in my daisy dukes to pouring water all over myself, I decided this was going to happen.

"If you don't, I will."

"I guess I need to figure out what to wear."

"We can go shopping. I know a great place."

"I don't have a lot of money."

She grinned. "Good thing the clothes you need are tiny."

I giggled. "Sure, why not?"

Adam opened his office door and pinned us with a stare. "I don't pay you ladies to stand around gossiping all night."

Roxie rolled her eyes, then blew Adam a kiss. I felt my eyes widen as she yanked me away toward the bar.

"That's our boss!" I hissed.

"He's a big ol' teddy bear."

"He looks more like a grizzly bear," I noted. He was tall, with broad shoulders, a narrow waist, and hair buzzed close to his head. He looked to be in his late twenties, but I couldn't be sure.

"His bark is worse than his bite."

"I wonder if all his ex-wives think so?"

"Good point." Roxie laughed. She picked up her tray and faced me. "Before you leave tonight, let's trade numbers."

I agreed and she moved off into the crowd.

I spent the rest of the night delivering drinks and smiling. It seemed the friendlier I was, the more tips I made. Still, I tried to remain professional. Well, as professional as I could in the center of a strip club.

A lot of these guys had a major case of grab hands. Good thing I moved fast.

By the time two a.m. rolled around, my feet hurt, my shirt was dry and kind of stiff feeling, and I really just wanted a shower.

Adam told me I was done for the night, but I had to fill out the paperwork before I could go. I went in the back and grabbed my bag, then plopped down at the end of the bar.

While I was waiting for Adam and the papers, I released my hair from the pony that was giving me a headache and pulled all the tips out of my apron and counted them. Two hundred dollars. Then I remembered the money from my dance, so I fished it all out of my bag and counted it. A hundred and fifty bucks. Not bad for almost falling on my face and making a fool out of myself.

Hottie bartender appeared in front of me. "Want me to cash out all those singles?"

"That'd be great. But I should wait and find out how much of this I have to share."

He shook his head. "We don't share tips here. What you get is what you earn."

"Seriously?"

"Yep. Adam says if the table hands you a tip, it's because they like you and not whatever drink you brought them. It's why the girls don't really have sections. It's kind of a free-for-all."

I nodded. It was kind of like a free-for-all.

I handed over my stack of cash. "It's three hundred and fifty. You can just give me twenties or whatever you have."

"Not bad for your first night," he said, then went over to the cash register and exchanged all my ones for larger bills.

When he came back, he handed me the cash and a glass of ice water with a straw in it.

"Thanks."

"What's your name, new girl?"

"I'm using Violet as my stage name."

His lips lifted. "Clever," he mused, reaching out to touch the purple strand in my hair.

"You got a real name, *Violet?*" Why is it that everything he said sounded like sex on a stick?

Or maybe it wasn't his words. Maybe it was the fact that his fingers were still playing with my hair.

"Harlow," I said, trying to hide the little tremor in my voice.

"Harlow," he repeated. It sounded like a purr that rumbled from deep inside him.

"How about you? You got a name?"

He was still twirling my hair along his finger and the simple, lazy movement was literally making my stomach quiver with some sort of anticipation.

"Cameron," he said, his voice low because he was leaning over the bar toward me. "Everyone calls me Cam."

"Are you a surfer, Cam?" I asked, my voice throaty and low. How is it that I tried the entire night to sound like that and never managed?

He cocked his head to the side. "How'd you know?"

I shrugged. "You look like a beach kind of guy." All tan muscles and messy blond hair.

"You think I'm hot."

"You seem to have a thing for my hair."

His movements stilled and he glanced at his fingers tangled in my hair. His eyes widened just a fraction and it made me think he hadn't realized what he was doing. It created a little fizzle of disappointment inside me because I liked the idea of him touching me because he liked it. I didn't want it to be some kind of weird accident.

"What can I say? My hands sometimes have a mind of their own."

The bottom dropped out of my stomach and something low in my abdomen clenched.

"Cam," Adam said from behind me. "Are you hitting on my new dancer?"

Cam pulled away, returning to me my personal space he'd been crowding. My body seemed to follow him, as if trying to be close to him again.

"You better watch out for this one, Violet. He's a real ladies' man."

I glanced back at Cam, arching an eyebrow.

He grinned.

"Here," Adam said, stacking some papers in front of me and handing me a pen. "When you're done, you can go. Be here tomorrow night to dance at seven."

I couldn't help but sneak little glances at Cam out of the corner of my eye as I wrote. Was it true? Was he a ladies' man? If he were, it would do me no good to be attracted to him. I wasn't the kind of girl that would stand in line for attention. I guess I wouldn't be surprised if he was. I mean, he worked in a strip club and his uniform was shirtless. Suddenly I understood why there were women in this club. All the bartenders were men and all of them were hot.

When Cam caught me looking, he smirked and I averted my gaze and finished up the paperwork. I picked it up to carry into Adam's office, but Roxie intercepted me.

"Taking that to the boss?"

I nodded.

"I'll do it." She reached out and took the papers.

"You don't have to do that."

"I want to."

There was something about the way she said it…
I gasped. "You have a thing for him?!"

She got this *who me?* look across her face, but
then she smiled. "Maybe a little crush."

"More like a big one." I teased.

She sighed. "It doesn't matter anyway. He won't
date the dancers. He doesn't mix business with
pleasure."

"I thought he was married."

"I doubt it will last; none of his marriages do."

"Is he damaged?"

"I just don't think he's found the right woman
yet."

"Well, if you ask me, he needs to stop getting
married until he actually finds her."

"Maybe he's a hopeless romantic." She sighed,
gazing toward his office door.

"Maybe he's a typical guy who thinks with the
brain inside his pants."

She snorted. "Yeah, you're probably right."

"Well, thanks," I said, gesturing to the papers.

She nodded. "Call me tomorrow and we'll meet
up before work. Get you some outfits."

She headed into Adam's office and I went
outside. Ty held open the door for me as I walked out
to the parking lot. "That was some dancing tonight,
Miss Harlow."

"I'm a complete disaster, Ty."

He chuckled. "You got the job, didn't ya?"

"Yep." I smiled, proud of myself. Passing an
audition to become a stripper might not be something
I should be proud of, but dammit, I was. It took a lot

of guts for me to do what I did tonight and I was able to hold on to my job without actually getting naked.

"See you tomorrow night, sugar."

I waved good-bye and went around the side of the building to the back of the lot where I was able to squeeze my car. The air was thick and humid even at this early hour. I lifted my hair up off my shoulders and tied it into a messy knot on the top of my head to keep it from sticking to my neck. I wanted a shower and my bed. If I made tomorrow night what I did tonight, I could pay off half my bills. Then I would just need to catch up on my rent and start paying toward my tuition.

I had to keep my school schedule on track. I had a four-year plan that included a bachelor's degree, and I fully intended to make it happen.

I unlocked my Toyota and climbed inside, anxious to turn on the air-conditioning. I slid the key in the ignition and turned. The engine turned over. The car did not start. I tried again. Same thing.

I groaned. "Not tonight," I said to the car.

Then I pumped the gas pedal (isn't that what you're supposed to do?) and tried again. That didn't work either.

I leaned my forehead against the steering wheel and considered my options. I could go look under the hood and try to fix whatever the problem was. Maybe it was something easy like something coming unplugged.

I climbed out of the car, popping the hood and staring down at the filthy, greasy engine. *Ew*. It was so dark that I could see practically nothing. What I could see didn't appear to be broken.

I laughed a little at my incompetence and let the hood fall back into place.

It was dark out here.

The parking lot was almost empty.

It was after two a.m.

I could call a cab. But that would eat into the money I needed to pay bills.

With a sigh, I trekked back to the door. Ty raised an eyebrow when he saw me again but opened the door for me. I looked around for Roxie, thinking maybe she could give me a ride home. But she wasn't on the floor. I glanced at Adam's office and the door was shut. If she was in there, I really didn't want to bother her. That seemed like some sort of violation of girl code.

"I thought you left?" Cam said, coming around the bar.

His black dress pants hung dangerously low on his hips, but were belted into place. Peeking just a little above his waistband was the thick band of his grey boxers. The lighter color drew my eye like a thief to an open bank vault.

"Is Roxie around?" I asked, forcing myself to look anywhere but at his narrow hips.

He shrugged. "Something wrong?"

"My car won't start."

"I'll look at it."

"I already did. It's too dark to see anything."

"You know about cars?" he said, his brows rising halfway up his forehead.

"Well, no."

He laughed, grabbed a black leather jacket, and went toward the door of the bar. "Come on."

I followed him out into the darkness and directed him to my traitor of a car. He popped the hood and bent over the engine. It was really hard not to notice how firm his butt looked in those pants.

"Turn the key, will ya?" he said, his head still out of sight.

I went and did what he asked, and the engine did nothing again.

"Battery's dead," he announced, slamming the hood.

I uttered a curse word.

"I'd give you a jump, but I brought my bike to work tonight."

"How did the battery die?"

"You leave your lights on or something?"

I glanced down. My lights were in the on position. "How did that happen?" I muttered. "Wasn't even dark when I came to work."

"I'll give you a ride."

I probably bumped it while I was sitting in here bouncing with nerves before my shift earlier. Geesh, today was not my day.

But then his words broke through the beating I was giving myself. "What did you say?"

"I'll give you a ride."

"Oh, you don't have to do that."

"Maybe I want to."

"Says the ladies' man," I quipped. It was more of a reminder to myself to not be taken in by that blond hair and dark stare.

"Say's the boss who's been married four times."

"Touché."

"It's right over there." He gestured to a black and silver crotch rocket against the building.

"I don't know," I murmured, climbing out of my car and chewing on my bottom lip.

"You ever been on a bike before?" Cam asked, slipping the leather jacket over his bare chest. Even still, I could see parts of his abs and the top of his boxers in the center where his jacket hung open.

I shook my head.

"This night is full of firsts for you, then, isn't it?"

I felt my cheeks heat a little at the undertones of his words. I won't lie; something warm began to swirl around inside me. "I can't believe he hired me," I mused.

"I knew he would. You've got this sweetness about you that no one else in that place has."

"I'm not sure that's a good thing."

"It's a good thing. Trust me."

Trust him. I didn't even know him. But I wanted to. I was tempted. Boy, was I ever tempted.

He pulled the bike away from the wall, rolling it forward and straddling the black seat. He looked so in control, so powerful sitting there with all that metal and steel between his legs.

"So what's it going to be, Harlow?" he said, a slight challenge in his voice. "You want a ride?"

If I didn't get on that bike, I would regret it forever.

I nodded and stepped forward.

4

He pulled a black helmet off the back of the bike and held it out. "Here."

"Where's yours?"

"This is mine."

I shook my head. "You take it."

He rolled his eyes and climbed off the bike, making sure it was steady before leaving it to stand in front of me. Without saying a word, he reached up and pulled the band out of my hair. Dark strands fell over my head and his arm, tickling my shoulders.

He held out the band, stretching it with his fingers so it was wide. "Here," he said, gesturing to my hand. I held up my arm and he linked our fingers, sliding the band over onto my wrist.

But he didn't pull away just yet.

Instead, he wrapped his fingers around mine, sliding down to circle my wrist where the pad of his thumb brushed over the thin, sensitive flesh on the underside.

"I like your hair down," he murmured, lowering my arm and his hand to step just a fraction closer so he could bury his nose in the hair that fell over my ear.

My heart was beating so hard that it was the only thing I could feel. Well, that and the way his even breathing tickled the soft strands and echoed into my ear. My thigh muscles clenched together and I stood stock still because I was afraid if I moved I would melt into a puddle at his feet.

Cam pulled back, releasing his gentle grip on my wrist and looked down. When our eyes met, I felt the crackle of desire surround us, and then he smiled. He had a dimple in his left cheek.

"I'll help you," he said, his voice brushing along my exposed nerve endings and making me shiver. "You cold?" he asked, frowning.

"No."

I caught the look of recognition in his eyes when he reached up and brushed the hair behind my ear. He knew exactly what he was doing to me. In fact, I would guess he enjoyed it.

Two could play that game.

I hooked a finger beneath the bowtie around his neck. "I like this," I said, trailing my finger along the fabric that wrapped around his neck.

"Yeah?" he asked after a moment, his voice tellingly hoarse.

"Mm-hmm."

"It's itchy."

I made a clicking sound with my tongue and slid my finger all the way around so my hand was caught between the leather of his jacket and the warm skin of his neck. His body stiffened just a little as my fingers brushed over him as I found the clasp that held the bowtie in place and undid it, causing it to fall away. Using my palm, I smoothed my hand around the base of his throat again and then pulled back to look up. "That better?"

He didn't say anything but swallowed thickly, and I gave him a little smile, tucking the bowtie in the pocket of his jacket. He cleared his throat and pulled the helmet down over my head. It was heavy and a little too big. I felt if I didn't hold my head perfectly straight, the weight of it would topple me over.

"I look like a bobble head." I complained as he adjusted the strap beneath my chin.

"A little," he agreed and smirked.

Before I could insult him back, he closed the face shield on the front and straddled the bike again.

"Climb on," he instructed.

Thank goodness I was wearing shorts. I swung my leg up over the side and sat down. The seat was narrow and not really comfortable. I held myself stiffly, trying not to slide into him, but the way the seat angled it was kind of hard not to.

I placed my bag between us and then he grabbed my legs just beneath the knees and pulled. My body came up against him all at once. My breasts pressed up against his back and it occurred to me that I never put my bra back on once I was finished working. He was completely solid all over, there was nothing but my thin tank and his jacket separating my skin from his, and... he was now sitting between my thighs.

The bike came to life beneath us, rumbling and vibrating my legs all the way up into the center of my crotch. Cam reached behind him, taking my arms and looping them around his waist, where the sensitive skin of my wrists brushed against his middle. When I thought he would pull away, he didn't, instead he flattened his palm against my hands, sandwiching them between the smooth skin that pulled taut over his ribs. His skin was warm, like it never lost the heat it soaked in during all his time in the sun.

"Hold on," he yelled over his shoulder, still pressing my hands against him before letting go and grabbing the handles.

The bike began to glide over the pavement, and I found my arms tightening around him just a little bit more. We moved slowly at first. He was very good at maneuvering the bike through the parking lot, and I began to relax a little. The nerves I initially felt when climbing on this bike dissolved a little with every passing second.

And then he turned onto the main road.

The bike quickly picked up speed. I squeezed my eyes shut against the blurry scenery around us. I wasn't sure I was meant to travel at this speed. All the tension in my body came back plus some, and I held myself rigidly, afraid if I even shifted once it would throw the bike sideways and we would barrel into oncoming traffic, or worse, fall over.

I didn't notice the way his body shook at first because everything on this bike was shaking—vibrating from the hum of the engine—but this was different. *He was laughing.*

"What?" I screamed and then squeezed my eyes shut, sure that just my talking was going to make us crash.

His shoulders shook more. "You're scared!" he yelled over his shoulder.

"Am not!" I yelled like a petulant five-year-old.

His hand, large and warm, covered mine where I was gripping at his chest and he gave it a light squeeze. I was about to yell at him for only driving with one hand when he spoke again. "I got you."

Three words.

How could three little words cause something inside me to bottom out and then swell with emotion?

I got you.

They weren't even particularly exciting words. But there was something about the way he yelled it while he covered my hand with his. It was like instead of asking me to trust him, instead of telling me not to be scared, he was *showing* me.

And I believed him.

My muscles relaxed; they quivered slightly from the exertion of being so tense. Suddenly, I realized I was plastered up against him. It seemed every part of my body touched him. I practically wrapped myself around his body in a giant bear hug. Even my ankles had hooked themselves around his calves.

If I hadn't been wearing such a massive helmet, I had no doubt that my cheek would be pressed against his back and my hair would be trailing behind us as he drove.

It was just one more reason to hate this helmet.

I opened my eyes and looked around, really looked.

Because of the late hour, the roads weren't filled with traffic like they usually were. All the shops, the tattoo parlors, the bars, and restaurants were lit up with bright neon lights and large signs. As we moved, the lights whipped by us, creating a blur of color in my line of sight.

The air outside was hot, but traveling like this, the wind pulled at my clothes and body. It brushed over my skin, creating goose bumps in its wake, and I huddled just a little bit closer to his warmth.

Just as I was starting to enjoy the ride, the bike downshifted beneath me and slowed as he turned off the main road and drove a short distance to an apartment building that rose up out of the concrete like some imposing force.

This wasn't my apartment.

Come to think of it, I hadn't even given him directions.

He stopped the bike in a spot by the curb and shut off the engine. I pried myself off his body and lifted up the face shield. "Where are we?"

"My place."

"You live here?" I asked nervously as he climbed off and turned to face me.

"On the third floor. I'd invite you in, but I'm not that kind of guy."

I snorted. I bet he wasn't.

He laughed and gently pulled the helmet off my head. My hands automatically went to my hair because I knew it was probably mashed to my head like I'd been wearing a hairnet.

"So I didn't kill you," he said, hooking the helmet on the side of the bike.

"You didn't bring me home either."

"I figured we could grab my car and go back to the bar. I can jump your car and then you'll be able to take it home. You might need it tomorrow."

Actually, I did need it. "You have a car and a bike?"

He pointed to a vintage mustang convertible parked next to the bike. It was cherry red with a white ragtop. "Yep."

Damn, I didn't know what was hotter—the bike or the car.

"I like it," I said, climbing off the bike. My legs felt funny, like the cells inside them were still vibrating—like they thought I was still riding on the bike. As I stood, I stumbled a little bit and fell against his chest. Automatically, his arms came up around my waist and I stood there in his embrace, completely dumfounded as heat rushed through my veins and scorched every active brain cell.

"Your legs will feel normal in a few." His voice was a mere whisper; he didn't have to talk loud because I was right up against him. He pulled back, still keeping his arms around me, and looked down. Our eyes met and the heat that had been rushing through me all drained into my stomach, pooling in the bottom of my belly and placing this heavy pressure down against my core.

I shifted, trying to get a little relief, but it made it worse because my body brushed against his hips.

Oh my God. I was acting like some hormonal teenager.

I stepped back and he let me go, and I rushed to put some much needed distance between us. I didn't know what was happening to my body, but it was losing its mind.

He pulled a set of keys out of his pocket and went around to unlock the passenger side of the Mustang. I climbed in and breathed a sigh of relief when the door closed behind me. We didn't speak on the way back to the Mad Hatter, and I busied myself with looking at everything but him.

When my car came into view, I wanted to scream with relief but decided that might be a little rude. He pulled the Mustang right up in front of my Toyota so the cables would reach from one battery to the other.

Before he climbed out of the car, I laid a hand on his forearm. He looked at me with a puzzled expression. "I really appreciate this, Cam," I told him. "You don't even know me and you're going out of your way in the middle of the night to help me."

"I'm getting something out of it too," he said slyly.

I lifted an eyebrow. "You are?"

He grinned. "Did I forget to mention that you owe me now?"

"I'm pretty sure this is the first I'm hearing about it."

He grinned and dammit, even in the dark his dimple caused my heart to melt. "You owe me, Harlow."

"What do you want?"

"I haven't decided yet."

Something about the way he said that caused a commotion to erupt inside my belly. It felt like there were tiny people in there doing jumping jacks. Very clumsy tiny people.

I stayed in the Mustang as he lifted the hood to both our cars and then retrieved the jumper cables out of his trunk. When they were connected, he knocked on the window and I looked over, my eyes colliding with the view of his defined abs. And yeah, his abs were really good-looking, but what made my hands clench was the little indentations on each side of his hips… you know that hollow indent that really in-shape guys got that led all the way to… well, to you know where.

I had this incredible urge to reach out and run my fingers over that part of him, to follow it to the very spot where it ended.

"Earth to Harlow," Cam called, leaning down and looking in the window.

I jumped like I was just caught robbing a bank and hurried to open the door. It swung open a lot easier than I thought and it smacked into Cam, making him grunt and double over.

"Cam!" I gasped, shutting the door and rushing to his side. "I'm such a klutz! Did I hurt you?"

I placed a hand on his shoulder and leaned down just as he was standing up, and his head caught my cheek.

When we smacked together, I shrieked and stumbled backward as searing pain cracked across my cheekbone.

A string of curse words fell from his lips and he grabbed my head, angling it back and turning my face so he could see me under the dim lights of the parking lot.

"How old are you?"

"Why, do I have wrinkles?" I asked, watching him study my face.

He rolled his eyes. "No, you do not have wrinkles."

"I'm twenty-one."

"How in the hell have you managed to keep yourself alive for twenty-one years?" he wondered as he smoothed the pad of his thumb across the tender flesh on my face.

It hurt, but I barely noticed. Every time he got close to me, it's like my brain went into some other universe, and in that universe everything consisted of only him.

His words followed my brain into that universe and I bristled. "I beg your pardon?"

He snorted. "Please. Like you don't know what I'm talking about."

"I've managed just fine!"

He dropped his hands—clearly deciding I wasn't that hurt—and smirked. "Since I've met you, you have tripped and fallen over a pair of flip-flops, fell onto a table, spilled beer all over two guys, managed to murder the battery on your car, fallen over while getting off my bike, hit me with the car door, and then slammed your face into my head."

"You hit me!" I growled, but in the back of my mind, I was thinking about that impressive list. Wow, I was practically a walking apocalypse. I reached up and brushed the still-stinging area and prayed I wasn't going to get a black eye. That would not be good for tips.

He palmed my face again, tilting my head back and studying it again. "Still hurt?" he asked low.

I nodded.

He bent, his breath brushing across my face before he pressed his lips not once, not twice, but three times over the area. They were feather-light kisses, but they mowed me over like a Mack truck.

"I'm sorry I hit you, baby. I'll make it better." Then he kissed me again.

I reached up and wrapped my fingers around his wrists. My heart thudded so unevenly it was hard to breathe. I felt lightheaded from his kisses, and all I could think about was getting just one more.

"Feel better?" he murmured as I clutched him to me. My eyes fluttered open and met his, which were so dark they looked like glittering black pearls.

I nodded just slightly. I did feel better... I couldn't even remember what hurt in the first place.

His lips quirked up in a half smile and then he kissed me again.

On the lips.

It was another one of those feather-light brushes, but oh my God, every single place inside me felt it. Something deep within me opened, something I hadn't even realized was closed... like there was this secret place and the combination to enter was his lips.

I made a soft sound as he lifted his head, so he came back, giving me just one more short taste.

His hands fell away from me and he stepped back, but I couldn't move. I couldn't even breathe. The only thing I could do was stand there and let the sensation of his kiss sink deep inside me until reality came rushing back.

I blinked. Kind of like I was waking up from some dream.

He watched me, an odd look on his face.

I was acting like a freak. Like someone who was starved for attention and would cling to any guy the first chance I got.

How pathetic.

I cleared my throat. "So are we going to do this or what?" I pushed past him and sat in the driver's seat of the Toyota. "Tell me when."

He went around and started up the Mustang, then signaled for me to turn the key. I did and nothing happened. So I tried again. I could hear him rev the engine of the Mustang, so I pumped the gas a bit and the engine finally turned over and purred to life.

I gave a shout of joy as the car rumbled and showed no signs of stalling.

Cam removed the jumper cables and closed both hoods and gave me a thumbs-up through the windshield.

I climbed out of my seat to fetch my bag from the floor of his car, but he met me halfway, extending it between us. "You should let the car run for a few more minutes just so the battery will charge up a little more."

"Think it will start tomorrow?" I worried.

"Should."

"Thanks again."

"Anytime."

He held up his finger, signaling for me to wait, and he jogged to his car, reached inside, and then came back to my side and extended a white business card to me.

"What's this?" I asked, taking the card.

"It has my number on it. If you get stranded or need a ride to work tomorrow, call me."

He was giving me his phone number. A little thrill went through me. I glanced down at the image of a surfboard sticking up out of a pile of sand.

Cam Malone
Custom Surfboards Made to Order

"You make surfboards?"

He nodded. "It's a hobby, but someday I hope to have my own surf and board shop."

"Wow, that's incredible."

"You like to surf?" he asked. I could see the passion for the sport in his eyes. I wanted to say yes so badly.

"Never been," I admitted.

"You live in Myrtle Beach and you've never surfed?" He gaped.

"I only moved here a couple years ago for college."

"Where you from originally?"

"Beaufort."

"There's beaches around there." He scoffed.

I shrugged. Surfing wasn't something I ever thought about doing. Until now.

"Of course, maybe it's better you haven't tried. You'd probably drown."

Ignoring his jest, I slid the business card in the back pocket of my cutoffs. "Guess I'll see you tomorrow night."

"Don't you want to know what you owe me?"

I braced myself for some wild proposition. "Yeah. What?"

"Come surfing with me."

That wasn't what I expected to hear. "Surfing?"

He nodded.

"Didn't you just say I would probably drown?"

His teeth flashed white in the dark with his quick grin. "You're not gonna drown. I'll be with you."

"What if I take you down with me?"

"You're not going to go down at all." He paused. "I got you."

Inwardly, I groaned. He said the magic words. "Okay, I'll go."

"I go every morning. Tomorrow?"

I gaped. "What time?"

"Usually around six."

"As in a.m.?" I raised an eyebrow.

He nodded.

"That's inhuman."

"I take it you aren't a morning person?"

"Not at all."

"You owe me."

I sighed. "Fine. But I can't tomorrow. It's already after three. I'll drown us both if I only get two hours of sleep."

"Day after tomorrow…" He tilted his head and flashed a crooked grin.

"Yeah, okay. But I have to work at ten. Will that be long enough?"

He seemed a little surprised. "You have another job?"

I nodded. "Yeah, this is my second job." I really needed the money.

"What do you do during the day?"

I blushed. "I run the snow cone cart over at Broadway at the Beach. It's just a summer job."

"What's your favorite flavor?"

"Pineapple."

"Original," he noted.

"How about you?"

"Cherry."

"A classic," I said as he moved closer, once again taking over my personal space.

"What can I say?" he murmured. "Classics never go out of style."

The way he stepped closer, staring at my lips, I thought he was going to kiss me again. A tremor of delicious anticipation moved through me as I waited to see if this kiss would be anything like the last.

But he didn't kiss me.

"I'll see you tomorrow, Harlow."

My eyes snapped open as he turned and walked back to his car.

I let out a shaky breath. I waited until he backed away before putting my car into drive and pulling out.

It took the entire drive home for my heart rate to return to normal.

5

I stopped for coffee on the way to work the next morning. Even at nine thirty in the morning, the temperatures were climbing, so I ordered an iced latte to go. Today was going to be ridiculously hot and I was going to swelter. Whatever possessed me to take a job that required me to be outside all day was beyond me. Oh, wait. I did know. It was the same reason I got a job as a stripper. I needed money.

I turned the AC on in my car as high as it would go and enjoyed the icy feeling on the surface of my skin because the minute I stepped outside again, I would do nothing but sweat the entire day.

Oh well. Between the sweating and the dancing, I was going to be in great shape by the end of the summer.

I parked my car and headed into the tiny snow cone headquarters—the little office off the shops where the snow cone carts and supplies were stored. I used my key to unlock the door and go inside to get what I needed for the day.

I worked quickly, stocking the cart with ice and flavorings. I made sure I had cash in the register and enough change to get me started. I tucked the folded umbrella beneath my arm, set my coffee, which was already sweating and turning watery, on top of the cart, and then headed to my spot near the water.

Broadway at the Beach is one of Myrtle Beach's main tourist attractions. It is sort of like an outdoor mall where people can shop, eat, and have a great time. It sits around a lake of sorts that is home to huge orange koi (that people can feed for a quarter) and ducks and birds of all kinds. People can also rent paddle boats and take captained boat rides.

There's also a mini golf place where a dragon pokes his head out of his lair every thirty minutes and blows out smoke and puts on a little show for people to watch. It's cute, but hearing it over and over all day stopped being cute for me a long time ago.

On the far end of Broadway lies Ripley's Aquarium. It's one of my favorite places to go. Even when it's packed with people (which is practically always). I always felt isolated and calm. All the water, the way the fish swam buoyantly through the water was very soothing to me after a very long day in the sun and crowds. Oh, and the massive air-conditioning inside helped too.

There is a wooden bridge on each end of Broadway, both connecting each side of the shops together. And it was on one of the ends of these bridges that I parked my cart.

I did so quickly and put up the umbrella so I could dive beneath it and at least be in the shade. My

Snow Cone Heaven T-shirt was already sticking to my skin and I rolled up the sleeves to my shoulders to allow more air to move around me. Then I tied the excess length of the shirt into a knot at my back.

Once the cart was ready, I sat down in my chair in the shade and sipped my coffee, people watching as the crowd began to grow.

I doled out a lot of snow cones that morning because the heat was so brutal. As I hid beneath the umbrella, I heard my cell ring from the back pocket of my white shorts.

"Hello?"

"Violet!"

I smiled. "Hey, Roxie." I knew it had to be her because who else would call me Violet?

"You ready for tonight?"

Umm, actually I wasn't. I was trying not to think about the fact I would be stripping every hour on the hour tonight. "Not really," I confessed.

"You will be after we go shopping. What time can you meet?"

I didn't get off until four. "Is four too late?"

"That should work."

"I'm at work now over at Broadway at the Beach. Can you meet me here later? By the aquarium?"

"Perfect. The place I want to go is right near there."

"It isn't Victoria Secret, is it?" I asked, dread forming in my stomach. There was a VS shop right near the aquarium. "I can't really afford that place right now."

"No one can afford that place," she muttered. "It's not. I know a local place. The woman pretty much sells for all the girls who work around here at all the strip clubs."

Her business must've been booming because it seemed there was a strip club on every corner here. After we agreed to meet, I disconnected the line and set my phone by the register. I glanced at my long-empty cup of coffee and sighed.

"Thirsty?" someone said in my ear from behind.

I screeched and shot a foot into the air. My hip caught the edge of the cart, and I groaned and grabbed the area where it hurt.

"There you go again," he drawled from behind.

I turned. It was Cam.

"Cam? What are you doing here?" I said, still rubbing at the spot on my hip.

"Want me to kiss it and make it better?" he asked, his eyes hidden behind a pair of mirrored aviator glasses. Even still, I felt the heat of his gaze linger on my legs.

Memories of last night crowded my mind and my skin tingled in memory of where he kissed me.

"No," I said firmly, even though the thought of his lips anywhere near that part of my body literally made my mouth run dry but caused other places on my body to become very moist.

He grinned and damn, he looked so good with a backward baseball cap on his head, the sunglasses, and a sleeveless dark-colored T-shirt and board shorts.

He even looked good in his flip-flops.

No man looked good in flip-flops.

Until now.

"Was on my way home from surfing and damn if I didn't get a craving for a snow cone."

I ignored the way my fingers slightly shook as I pulled open the ice bin and packed some fluffy shaved ice into a striped paper cup.

I told myself I leaned a little farther into the ice bin because the cold felt blissful against my heat-tortured skin. It had nothing to do with the fact I was trying to compose myself before facing him again.

When I couldn't delay any longer, I pulled up and closed the lid, reaching for the cherry-flavored syrup. "How were the waves this morning?"

"Righteous."

I laughed. "That is such a surfer dude thing to say."

"How do you stand this heat all day?" he asked, taking the red-drenched icy treat from me.

"Some day's are harder than others."

"Today?" He tilted his head and took a bite of the red ice, ignoring the spoon.

"Today's no picnic." I admitted. "But I only have a couple more hours."

"What time you get off?"

"Four. Then I'm meeting Roxie. She's going to take me shopping for tonight."

He paused in his inhaling of the snow cone. "I love my job."

I laughed. Another customer approached with two children, and I quickly made three rainbow-colored cones and made change for them. When they walked away, I turned back to Cam, but he was gone.

Disappointment made me sigh as I flung myself back into my chair. From across the way, the dragon poked its head out of its lair and let out a roar. I rolled my eyes. This heat was making me grouchy.

A few minutes later, a giant plastic cup appeared in front of my face. It was filled with light-yellow lemonade and several round lemon slices. The cup was packed with ice and liquid and looked so refreshing that I actually whimpered.

I stared at the cup, transfixed, telling myself my mind was conjuring up mirages because I was so heat exhausted. As I watched, the cup came closer until it pressed against my cheek and then my forehead. I sighed. That felt so incredibly good.

Then the cup slid down until the straw poked at my lips and I pulled it between them, taking a long pull of the sweet yet tart liquid. I felt its icy temperature plunge all the way down my throat and then spread through my stomach, coating it in a chilled wave.

I groaned because it was probably the best drink I ever had. The lemon was perfectly refreshing and the ice was crispy cold.

"You keep making those sounds and I'm going to bring you one of these every single day."

My eyes shot open and I turned. Cam smiled and pulled the cup back so I didn't knock it out of his hands.

Well, wasn't I embarrassed? I was also an idiot, thinking that my lemonade cup was a mirage.

"You brought that for me?"

He nodded.

"Thank you. I really needed that. I forgot to put my extra water in the cart before I came out here."

"You owe me again," he said, reaching around to set the lemonade beside the register.

I crossed my arms over my chest. "I'm already going surfing with you. What else do you want?" I said it like I was annoyed, but I wasn't. The thought of owing Cam anything made me giddy, and I secretly couldn't wait to hear with what he came up with next.

"Haven't decided."

I arched an eyebrow.

He stepped forward and pressed a kiss to my hairline. "Drink your lemonade while it's still cold."

I didn't reply because he was touching me, and all I could think about was how he smelled like the ocean and coconut oil and how his lips felt cool against my skin.

"I'll see you tonight," he said and then turned and walked away.

He didn't even look back.

Which was probably a good thing because I couldn't tear my eyes away until he was out of sight. I turned back to the lemonade, staring at it while I climbed back into my chair. The outside of the cup was already sweating and I watched as a drop of water made its way down the side. Then something around the side of it caught my eye.

I leaned forward, picked up the cup, and spun it around to look.

There in the frosty perspiration Cam had drawn a heart.

*　*　*

HushHush was located just a few miles from Broadway at the Beach, but it could have been a hundred miles away because here it was a lot less touristy and more of an area where the locals would hang when they didn't want to deal with crowds and out-of-towners.

It was a little shop nestled between a bakery and a tobacco store. It was tasteful out front, with purple drapes lining the windows and just a small sign on the door with the name of the shop.

Roxie grinned like a pirate who found treasure when she yanked open the door and motioned for me to go inside.

The inside was not as tasteful or… shall we say… discreet as the outside, and part of me felt like a giant nun because I was slightly embarrassed.

The walls were all painted a deep shade of plum and appeared made of some sort of stone. The dark color made the inside feel intimate and cave-ish. There were large posters hanging on the walls in gaudy gold frames. The posters were all of women in sexy lingerie lying across unmade beds, sitting provocatively on chairs or other women, or draping themselves along a stripper pole.

In a couple of the posters toward the back, the women were completely topless.

From the ceiling, a chandelier hung in the same gaudy gold color, dripping in crystals. In between the posters were floating shelves, all with mannequin heads sporting wigs in all colors and styles. There was a makeup counter in the back and a leopard-print velvet sofa in the center of the room perched atop a white faux fur rug.

And everywhere else there were clothes.

If you called the garments that hung on the racks and bars coming out of the walls clothes.

To me it looked more like really fancy, really tiny bikinis.

From beside me Roxie giggled and I glanced at her. "I love newbies," she said with a grin.

So it wasn't just me. She knew this place was over the top too; she was just used to it. I guess if I came here often enough, the décor and nakedness surrounding me would lose some of its surprise.

"Honey," Roxie called toward the back. "I'm here."

A few minutes later, a woman with dark skin and a bright-red wig came out of the back. She wasn't a small woman, standing probably close to six feet tall with a wide build that appeared to enjoy a lot of southern cooking. Her wig was styled in an ultra-sleek bob that ended just at her shoulders and was the kind of red you might get out of a Kool-Aid packet.

She was dressed in a loose golden caftan that shimmered when she moved, and she had a ring on almost every finger and the biggest, happiest smile I'd ever seen anyone wear.

"Roxie, girrrlllll," the woman named Honey purred. "You are looking good."

"You too, Honey, you too."

Honey's eyes turned to me.

"Honey, this is my new friend Violet. She's brand new at the Mad Hatter."

The woman's brown eyes lit up and she lunged at me, taking me into a huge bear hug. "Welcome, Shug," she exclaimed. "Any friend of Roxie's is a friend of Honey's."

She pulled me back and looked me over. "You need a little more meat on your bones. Men want something to grab on to when they reach out their hands."

I felt my cheeks bloom with bright pink splotches.

Honey laughed. "It's all right, Shug. I keep telling Roxie here the same thing."

Roxie nodded sagely.

"So what kind of things do you need?" she asked me, looking me over again.

"I—" I began, but Roxie cut me off.

"She needs everything."

Honey made an mmhmm sound and headed for the racks. Roxie and Honey began talking real fast and holding up scraps of fabric, debating and laughing about everything they said. Roxie held up a couple things to herself while Honey kept adding to the mountain in her hand, and I began to worry about how much all that barely there fabric was going to cost me.

Then she held up a G-string.

"No!" I said, butting into the conversation that I had purposely stayed out of. "I am not wearing any of that butt floss."

"Butt floss?" Honey said and looked at me with wide eyes.

Roxie began giggling and then Honey burst out in a huge rowdy laugh. The two of them laughed for a good ten minutes. I mean, I started to get bored. I don't really know what was so funny about sticking a string up your butt crack.

When they finally stopped laughing, Honey put down the G-string and announced she wouldn't add "butt floss" to the pile.

"I don't want anything too skimpy either," I told her.

She stared at me like I had three heads.

"I want to leave something to the imagination. I want people to wonder what I'm going to show when

I get on the stage. I don't want to be trashy," I finished, feeling self-conscious. I didn't want either of them to think I was insulting them, because I wasn't, but I had my own personal limits I wanted to adhere to.

"Violet is your stage name, isn't it?" Honey asked, looking at me freshly again.

I nodded.

"Your real name Harlow?"

"How'd you know that?" I asked, looking at Roxie. Roxie shrugged.

"Ty told me there was new girl, a Miss Harlow, at the bar and he told her not to be trashy."

I smiled. "You know Ty?"

Roxie giggled.

"Child, I'm Ty's better half."

I tried not to gape. "You and Ty are married?"

"Did you think that chocolate bar of a man was walking around single?" she said, waving her finger in my face.

I hadn't really thought about it at all, actually. But now that I did… "No, I suppose not."

"Mmhmmm," she said and thrust the pile of clothes at me. "Get your skinny butt in the back and try some of this on."

I hurried toward the back, stopping to glance inside the makeup case, hoping to spy some body shimmer powder.

Only this wasn't a makeup case.

It was full of… um… personal massagers.

One of them was so big and bumpy looking that I was sure there was no way in hell anyone could think it felt good *in there.*

After that thought, I spun away and ran behind the curtain where the dressing room was.

Half the stuff in the pile I brought back here I couldn't figure out how to put on. A few pieces were entirely see-through and one was made of what I strongly suspected was fishing net. Those all stayed on the floor.

I realized a stripper had to look sexy. I realized a stripper had to be desirable and entertaining.

But this stripper had her own ideas.

As I dug through the clothes, for some reason the image of my ex-boyfriend flashed through my memory. *You're nothing but a tease,* he'd taunted me the day I confronted him about spreading rumors about me through the entire school. I don't know why my brain decided to bring that up at this moment, but I was sort of glad it did… because it gave me an idea.

An idea that I sort of already tried out and it had worked.

If it worked once, then why wouldn't it work again?

I smiled at myself in the mirror and pulled out a couple things from the bottom of the pile. I held up a black bustier with a black zipper right down the front and nodded my head. I piled it on the round ottoman in the dressing area and laid out black thigh-highs and garters to hold it up. Then I fished around until I found a pair of black panties with little patches of black lace all over them.

It was sexy as hell, it left a little to the imagination, but at certain angles, I had no doubt it gave a little peek. Then there was the zipper… I could have all kinds of fun with a zipper.

Next I pulled out a silver bodysuit. It looked like a simple one piece bathing suit except right over the breasts was purple star-shaped see-through material. It had a sheen to it, and when I moved the outfit, the stars caught the light and shimmered.

I wondered how revealing it would be, so I hurried and put it on, then turned to look at myself in the mirror.

Shock made me do a double-take.

The material was thick and tight. It held in all my curves, smoothed them out, and the soft cups acted like a push-up bra and gave me some hella cleavage. You could see a little bit of nipple through the stars, but I supposed it wasn't totally embarrassing.

It was very high cut around the thigh and when I turned to look at my butt, I gasped a little because there was more see-through purple material back there. In the shapes of hands. It looked like someone was grabbing my butt.

"I want to see something!" Roxie demanded.

I pulled the curtain back and strutted out and put my hands on my hips. "What do you think?"

"I think you have to buy that," Roxie said.

"Chiillld," Honey sang, coming from the front. "I got something for that." She appeared seconds later with a deep-purple wig. Before I could protest, she slid it down over my head, tucking my dark hair up underneath and smoothing it out.

She made a tsking sound when she pulled back to look at her handiwork.

I turned and looked in the mirror. The wig hit me at my chin and curled under slightly. There was a heavy row of bangs that fell just above my eyes. My blue irises practically glowed with all the purple around them and my lips seemed to look pinker.

Roxie appeared in the mirror beside me. "It's perfect."

"You don't think the wig is too much?"

"Definitely not. Especially not with just the spotlight on when you're on stage."

I studied it a second longer and decided she was right. This wasn't an outfit I would ever step outside in. In fact, I would probably bury it in the back of my closet until I had to take it to work, but this would be amazing on stage—because that's where an outfit like this belonged. And it fit exactly the kind of look I was going for… not too much, but not too little.

I smiled secretly to myself.

Violet was going to be a tease.

6

Cam was climbing off his crotch rocket when I parked at the back of the lot like I did the night before. This time I made sure my headlights were off and stayed that way. Although, part of me was tempted to leave them on just so Cam would have to jump my car again.

Once I climbed out of the car, I reached into the back to pull out a canvas black duffle filled with my new items from Honey's shop. I was pretty happy with the choices I made. A couple of them were a little more risqué than others, but I decided to try and look at it like a business, as nothing but a job, and hopefully that would make parading around in my undies more bearable.

Cam leaned against the side of my car when I shut the back door and slung the bag over my shoulder. It was the first time I'd seen him completely covered.

My eyes kind of missed the skin.

He was dressed in his black work trousers, black shoes, some sort of black shirt, and a black leather jacket. It was a motorcycle jacket with zippers on the pockets and a collar that slipped up around his square jaw.

His arms were folded across his chest and he looked me up and down. Suddenly, I wished I were wearing something other than a pair of light-blue cotton shorts and a striped baby tee.

At least my hair was done. I'd taken time to curl it after my shower and it fell in loose spiral waves all the way down to my shoulders. I decided to keep my makeup to the minimum because I figured no one would be looking at my face anyway. Just a coat of lipstick and some extra mascara would hopefully dress me up enough.

"Figured I'd make sure you remembered to shut off your lights and didn't trip and fall on your way inside," he said, watching me lazily.

"Ha. Ha," I said, swinging the bag and hitting him in the middle.

He made an oomph sound and caught it, tugging it away and carrying it for me.

"We still on for tomorrow morning?"

"A debt is a debt," I said, smiling.

"Want me to pick you up?"

"Sure, I'll probably still be half asleep anyway."

"You can give me your address when we get inside."

I nodded.

"You ready for tonight?"

I let out a breath. My nerves had been building the closer the clock crept to seven o'clock. "I don't think I'll ever be ready for this."

"You know the guys here… they aren't allowed to touch you. If any of them crosses the line, you yell for Ty or one of the other bouncers."

"Okay."

He stopped and grabbed my arm, pulling me around gently. "I mean it, Harlow. If anyone makes you uncomfortable, you yell. If you can't find a bouncer, you yell for me, okay?"

It made me even more nervous, the warning of sorts he was giving me. "Have one of the girls been… hurt before?"

He let go of my arm and tucked a strand of hair behind my ear. "No. Adam has always been really proactive about keeping everyone safe."

"Then why the need for the ominous warning?"

"Shit," he swore and pushed a hand through his hair. "I didn't mean to scare you. I just wanted you to know that…" His voice faded and then he swore again. "I just—"

"You just wanted me to know you got me," I whispered, feeling my chest swell a little.

Relief crept into his eyes and he smiled. "Exactly."

I felt my own lips tilt up. "Yeah, I know."

Inside the bar, I wrote my address on a napkin and slid it across the bar as Cam washed some glasses and stocked the bar.

There was already a good crowd in here, and I knew by night's end the place would be packed. With fifteen minutes until I had to be on stage, I went backstage and set my bag at my little dressing table. I unpacked my cosmetics and then pulled out the wig with the white mannequin head and set it in front of the mirror. It had been a gift from Honey. The wig was over my budget, but she made me take it, saying that it was made just for me.

Her place might have been over the top, but she was just right. I smiled thinking about the way she called me "Shug."

The girls were all in the back, getting dressed and talking amongst themselves. I felt a little awkward, like I didn't belong, but I was grateful that I had my clothes and things to busy my hands with so I wasn't just standing around like a little lost lamb.

Most of the girls back here were all gorgeous and tall with model-like bodies. In fact, some of them probably could be models. I wondered why they didn't do that instead, but it wasn't my place to ask. After all, I was doing this too.

None of them seemed bothered by showing so much of their skin, either. Heck, a couple of the girls walked around completely topless and wearing only a thong. It made me begin to doubt my plan and my outfit choices… My clothes had a lot more fabric than these girls'.

I decided to just give it a shot (and go a little heavier on the makeup). If it didn't work out tonight, maybe Adam would just let me serve tables, and if he didn't, I could always quit and find another job.

Feeling a little better, I slipped into the black outfit with the corset and thigh-high stockings. I struggled a little with the garter, but one of the girls named Candy offered to help me, and in no time I had them strapped on and was stepping into my black stilettos (the only pair of really nice shoes I owned). The last thing I did was clip the purple hair extension in my hair and give it a quick curl to match the rest.

Roxie wasn't here yet to give me a pep talk, so it was up to me to get my booty out onto that stage and perform. Thank goodness she lent me one of her mix CDs with music from a set of routines she hadn't performed in several years. It was already with the DJ, and I just told him to play the songs in order as I came out on stage to do my routines.

And then it was my turn. Candy motioned me to the stage behind the curtain, I was shaking and so nervous I felt like I was going to throw up right there in front of everyone.

I still didn't know what I was going to do.

The DJ announced me and then the spotlight clicked on over the center of the stage, illuminating a circle of light on the floor. Everything else around it was completely dark. The crowd in the bar had quieted to a low murmur, and I could hear the pounding of my own heart.

The music started playing.

It was something with a heavy beat that made my hips want to swing a little more than usual. This could work.

Taking a deep breath, I stepped out from behind the curtain, at the last moment grabbing a white wooden chair and dragging it behind me with one hand as I went. I did my best to slink along the floor, to take long, drawn-out steps and really bump out my hips when I moved.

When I got to the circle of light, I moved around it so I dragged the chair into the center and set it down with the back facing the crowd. I was still in the dark.

The music picked up a little, thumping a little harder, the intensity growing, and I stepped into the light, keeping my back to the crowd. Then I spread my legs wide, planted my stilettos on the floor, and bent, letting my hands touch the floor. Then quickly my butt sank down, and as I stood, I pushed it out so everyone got an eyeful of the slightly see-through panties.

A couple guys whistled and then I spun. I grabbed the back of the chair and straddled it, gyrating my hips like I was riding a wild bull. Then I reached up for the zipper, lowering it between my breasts.

I went on for several moments, parading around the stage, especially the part that jutted out into the crowd. I even stomped the toe of my high heel down on a nearby table and, feeling brave, leaned down and licked my leg.

Seriously? Who thinks this is hot? the inner girl in me said.

They do, another voice answered. Apparently, a dirty ho had taken up residence within me without my knowledge.

Dirty ho was right, though. Some guy shoved a twenty in the top of my stocking.

On impulse, I grabbed him by the hair (I was taller than him because I was on stage) and towed him back, and the men went nuts. Then I shimmied my still pretty covered chest in his face and then shoved him away.

He fell to his knees and put his hand over his heart.

Oh please, said my inner voice.

Undo your zipper, urged the dirty ho.

I took her advice and slid it a little farther down. Then I took a finger and trailed it all the way down between my breasts and back up again.

As the song winded down, I did a few more shimmies and shakes and then walked toward the back of the stage near the chair.

As the last notes of the song played, I climbed on the chair, stood up, and put my back to the crowd. Then I undid the rest of the zipper, slipping the corset so it was around my wrists, not even on my body anymore.

I couldn't even hear the pounding of my heart over the whistling and catcalls.

I tipped my head back, like I was going to spin around and show them the goods… and then the song ended and the spotlight went out.

Darkness completely concealed me.

I let out a huge breath and hurried to zip the corset back around me.

I left the chair where it was and collected all the money from the stage and then ran behind the curtain.

Roxie stood there waiting. "Damn, Violet."

"Was it okay?" I worried as we moved backstage. I hadn't shown a single glimpse of my really private parts.

"Are you kidding? I've never seen men so enthralled by a woman who was still wearing clothes."

I laughed.

But then I caught a look at her face in the brighter light backstage. "What's wrong?"

"Nothing,"

"You look like you've been crying."

"It's no big deal."

"I know we just met and all, but if you ever need to talk, I'll listen."

Roxie smiled. Her long, nearly black hair fell over her shoulder. "Thanks."

I nodded as she moved away to get ready for her routine. I wondered if she was late for the same reason her eyes were a little puffy. But I wasn't sure I should press the issue. I mean, she might be showing me the ropes around here, but that didn't mean she wanted to confide in me.

I shrugged it off and went to check myself in the mirror and decided to just wear this outfit while I served for the hour. Instead of just shoving my cash in my bag and letting it lay back here, I straightened it all out, folded it, and put it in the pocket of the little black apron that I tied around my waist. I would rather have it on me than just sitting back here. I didn't think the girls would take it, but I didn't know them and I wasn't about to trust them.

Roxie was putting on some barely there spandex number when I ducked out of the room to head for the bar.

Cam waited with a tray full of drinks. I smiled when I saw him and my heart skipped a beat. I couldn't help but wonder if he liked my dance, if he thought it was sexy.

I grabbed for the tray as he leaned way over the bar and reached out his hand. Using his thumb, he swiped along my lower lip. "Lipstick," he said only loud enough for me to hear.

His touch sent little delicious shivers racing down my back. "Thanks."

"Anytime, gorgeous."

After that, the bar got really busy, really fast. I didn't have time to talk to anyone, including Roxie. I was so busy laughing and smiling and serving drinks that the hours went by without me even thinking about my next dance.

Each one was similar to the first one, but all my outfits changed, the music changed, and I tried to move around to different tables and places. One time I even sat in a man's lap. The whole time I did it, though, my mind screamed for me to find the hand sanitizer when I got up.

For my final dance, I repeated the one from the night before, with the cut-offs and the white tank top. Except this time I didn't spill a pitcher of beer; I only poured water over myself.

I made six hundred dollars just from dancing. I made another two hundred from serving drinks. I was practically giddy with the fact I made eight hundred dollars *in one night*.

I barely made that in an entire month at the snow cone cart.

Did I like this job?

No.

Would I admit to anyone that I was a stripper?

Probably not even at gunpoint.

Was I going to keep doing it?

Hell yes.

Once my shift was over, I changed into my cotton shorts and baby tee, finally slipping off the stilettos (my feet were officially dead) and getting comfy with my flip-flops. I used a face wipe to take off most of my makeup and then pulled my hair back in a high ponytail. It made me feel more like me and less like Violet.

I was beginning to think I was creating some sort of alter ego for myself with Violet, the more outgoing, crazy me. Or maybe I was just trying to find a way to deal with the fact I was a stripper.

On my way out, I stopped in the bathroom to wash my hands, and Roxie was in there, on her cell, and she was saying, "Why should I be the one to move out when you're the man-whore!"

The line was silent for a second and then she snorted. "Fine! I don't want to live there anyway. The whole place is probably infested with herpes!"

She hit a button on the screen and made a sound, then spun, her eyes going wide when she saw me.

"I'm sorry, I didn't know that anyone was in here," I stuttered, trying to cover the fact I pretty much just eavesdropped on her conversation.

"It's fine."

I moved to the sink and washed my hands. When I grabbed a couple paper towels, she said, "I caught my boyfriend in bed with some nasty skank and now he wants me to move out."

"He wants you to move out?"

"He says because I'm the one who broke it off, I should be the one to leave."

"What a douche bag."

"Right?" She half-smiled. "This isn't the first time I caught him cheating, but it's going to be the last. He thinks because I'm a stripper he doesn't have to be faithful or something. He thinks he doesn't have to respect me."

"You're so much better than that," I told her.

"Yeah. I know." She gave me a watery smile. "I haven't even loved him for a long time. He's just really good at getting me to stay."

"Well, if you keep staying, then you might miss a really great guy when he comes along."

"You think there are any good guys left out there?"

"I sure as hell hope so."

She laughed.

"Hey, why don't you move in with me?"

She looked up. "Really?"

I nodded, getting excited. "It would be perfect. I used to have a roommate, but she graduated in the spring and left. Starting next month, I was going to have to pay all the rent and everything by myself. Which means I was going to have to move, but if you move in, I wouldn't have to."

"How much is rent?"

"It would be five hundred a month for each of us. We can split the cable, but all the other utilities are included."

"Are you sure you don't mind?"

"Are you a big partier?"

"No."

"Do drugs?"

"Gross. But I do drink occasionally."

"Are you a morning person?" I asked, inwardly groaning at having a roommate who wakes up at the crack of dawn to bang around in the kitchen.

"Are you kidding? I work 'til three a.m. every night. My idea of morning is noon."

"When can you move in?" I asked.

She squealed. "Is tomorrow too soon?"

"Nope. If you want to come by tonight just to see the place before we make it official, you can. If you like it, I'll be sure to tell the landlord and you can drop by and sign the lease and get some keys tomorrow."

"Let me just make sure it's okay if I leave too and then I'll follow you to your place."

At the bar, Cam had a water with ice and a straw waiting for me. "Do I owe you for this too?" I asked as I reached for the drink.

"Nah, this one's on the house." He winked. "Hey, I seem to have lost the napkin with your address on it. I probably accidentally threw it away. Will you write it down again for me?"

"I don't know. Seems to me if you had really wanted it, you wouldn't have lost it."

His eyes narrowed. "Maybe I wouldn't have been so distracted if someone hadn't been strutting around half naked all night."

"If the sight of a half-naked woman distracts you, I think you are in the wrong line of work."

"Harlow," he growled.

"Cam," I growled back.

He leapt over the bar... like right over it. I made a little squeal and a couple of the people still lingering inside glanced our way. But we must not have been exciting enough (or maybe it was because I was overdressed now) because they looked away in seconds.

Cam backed me up so my shoulders were pinned against the bar and his arms rested on either side of my head, creating a cage. He was no longer wearing the motorcycle jacket—only that bowtie and trousers—and I stared at the way the muscles in his shoulders bunched with his movements.

A deep craving slammed into me and it wasn't for a cheeseburger or a donut. It was for him. Was it possible to crave another human being? I looked at his lips and the way they moved as he spoke. But I didn't hear a word that came out of his mouth.

He snapped his fingers in front of my face, and I looked up. "What?"

"What's the matter with you?"

I put my hands on his chest and shoved. He didn't budge. He smiled and leaned closer, his breath fanning out across my cheek and his lips grazing my temple. "I have ways of getting what I want, you know," he whispered.

I swallowed, desire curling up from deep inside me and saturating every part of my body. I didn't really know what to do with so much of it literally weighing me down. I was supposed to be the tease and here I was the one being taunted. By him. By my own body. By needs I'd never had before. "You do?"

"Oh yes. And if you aren't careful, you're going to find out all about my ways."

He stroked my collarbone with his finger.

I bit down on my lower lip. "I'll give it to you," I whispered.

His chuckle was rich and warm against my ear. Then he pulled back and slid a pen out of his pocket and handed it to me.

I turned away, grabbing the first napkin I saw, and scrawled my address with shaking hands.

When I handed it to him, he slid it into his pants pocket and smiled. Then he rubbed the back of his neck with one hand and peeked up at me with boyish charm written all over his face. "You know, part of me is disappointed that you gave in so easy."

"Well, since my address is in your pocket, I still say you came out on top."

Roxie appeared and lifted her eyebrows at how Cam and I stood so close. I glanced back at him. "See you tomorrow?"

"Wear your bathing suit."

I nodded and slid away from him, grabbing up my bag and heading for the door with Roxie hot on my heels.

Out in the parking lot, she gave me a long look.

"What?" I asked her.

"You know what." She grinned. "You and Cam?"

"We're just friends."

"Right. And I'm the Easter Bunny."

"You are! Where do you keep your tail?"

She laughed. "Well, I don't even care now what the apartment looks like."

"No?"

"Nope. I'm moving in purely for the entertainment of watching you and Cam. I can't wait to see what happens."

I had to admit, I wanted to see too.

7

Pounding on the front door of my apartment made me groan and roll over to look at the clock. Bleary eyed, I squinted at the little red numbers.

Six a.m.

"It does exist," I murmured to myself as the pounding continued.

I stumbled out of bed, pushing the hair off my forehead and trudging toward the door. I yanked it open and peered into the hallway.

"I changed my mind. I'm not going," I said and then swung the door shut and went back to bed.

I heard the sound of the door opening and closing behind me, but I was too tired to care. I crawled back onto the mattress and curled up on my side, pulling the covers to my chin. Didn't he know this hour of the morning/night was what was wrong with half of America today? Forcing people to get out of bed at ungodly hours only made them cranky.

I was slipping back into blissful sleep when I felt the bed dip with new weight. "Go away," I murmured.

I felt the blankets being tugged away and I tried to grasp them back, but it was too late. The covers were gone and the cool air brushed over my skin.

"I. Will. Punch. You." I growled.

He laughed. "Aren't you a little ray of sunshine in the morning?"

I swung at him. But seeing as how my eyes were closed and I was lying down, my aim wasn't good. Okay, my aim sucked.

He caught my fist and pulled it behind me. My body rolled and I found myself lying on my back with him looming over me.

He smelled really good. Like coffee and the sea.

I probably smelled like dragon breath.

"What's it gonna take to get you out of this bed?"

"An act of God."

Something large and very warm settled on my leg just above my knee. My eyes remained closed, but every cell in my body went on high alert.

Slowly, his hand slid higher, leaving a trail of warmth in its wake, until the pads of his fingers brushed over the inside of my thigh. I didn't mean to moan.

But I did.

His touch was like my kryptonite. Even the faintest, most accidental contact with him made every single living, breathing cell in my entire body explode with desire.

"Do you like that?" he murmured. His hand hadn't gone up any farther, but he continued to caress the sensitive flesh just inside my leg.

I felt him settle further onto the bed and then he lifted his hand. Sorrow oozed deep inside me at the loss of the contact I so desperately wanted.

But then his hand returned. His fingers dragged across the exposed skin of my belly between my boxers and the tank, which had ridden up.

My body was utterly relaxed, still from sleep and now from his gentle caress. I wouldn't have been able to run if a bomb landed in the living room. And then his fingers grew braver, finding the hem of my shirt and slipping beneath it.

I forgot to breathe as he traced the outline of my rib cage and dragged his nails gently across my abdomen. My nipples hardened into ultra stiff pebbles, and my breasts began to ache in a way they never had before. Without thinking, I arched up a little, trying to give his hand some direction, trying to get him just a little bit higher.

He paused, just slightly, as if he were debating on how far he was willing to go. And then his hand started moving again, until he palmed my breast completely.

"Harlow." My name on his tongue was like pollen to a bee. "Is this okay?"

"Mmmm," was all I could manage.

"Look at me," he commanded, his voice a little less seductive.

My eyes opened, looking into his deep, chocolate irises. "Is it okay to touch you here?"

"Yes."

His hand started to move then, and my eyes fluttered closed. He moved his hand in a circular motion, kneading the tender tissue and flicking his thumb over my tingling nipple. When he was done with one, he moved to the other, doing the exact same thing—kneading and moving, playing with my nipple until it almost hurt with need.

And then he lifted the shirt, air brushing across my overheated skin, and I felt his stare. I felt his eyes taking in every inch of me. I knew I was likely swollen with the blood that had rushed to the point of contact, almost like even the red liquid wanted to be close to him as well.

And then his mouth closed over the nipple closest to it. He latched on and swirled his tongue around the peak and nipped at it with his teeth.

I moan ripped from my throat as I squeezed my thighs together, feeling moisture pool between my legs, slicking my body for something it wholly wanted.

He kissed every inch of my chest, lavishing attention on both of my girls like a dying man in need of his final meal. At some point, my hands found their way into his hair and I clutched at his scalp, holding him still yet urging him on.

When my hips started to move restlessly, he lifted his head.

I opened my eyes and looked at him. His lips were slightly swollen. His eyes were so dark they looked like the moonless midnight sky.

He lay down, putting his arms on either side of my body so he was mostly on the mattress but partly covering me. Using his hands, he brushed the hair away from my face and then he kissed me.

It wasn't like the first time, the feather-light, barely there kisses. This was the kind of kiss I read about in books, the kind of kiss that ended epic movies and completely altered the world as you knew it.

His tongue delved deep into my mouth, as if he couldn't get close enough, as if he wanted to climb inside me and do things to my body that no man had ever done before. His lips were insistent, but not rough, the kiss moist, but not wet. Our mouths didn't separate, not one time; we didn't break contact. We just kissed—endlessly, deeply, feverishly.

I clutched at his back, pulling him even closer, sucking his upper lip into my mouth and running my tongue over its softness. He moaned so I did it again. He gathered me just a little bit closer and the hard ridge in his shorts wasn't to be missed. I could feel it pressed against the side of my hip and the ache inside me intensified.

My chest started to squeeze and it momentarily distracted me, so I managed to suck in just enough oxygen to keep my lungs happy.

Cam stilled his lips and pulled back, resting his forehead against mine. Both of us breathed heavily, our chests pressed together.

"Good morning," he said, his voice thick and deep.

My hips lifted at the sound and the inner muscles of my vagina clenched. "Hi."

"Do you kiss everyone that shows up at your door at six in the morning like that?"

"Just you."

"I'm one lucky bastard."

I giggled.

He pushed off me and stood, adjusting his shorts and T-shirt. "The beach is waiting."

I groaned. He hooked me around the ankle and pulled me across the sheets. "I brought you coffee."

"Okay, then."

He chuckled and pulled me onto my feet. My head felt dizzy, like I drank too much the night before, only I hadn't drunk anything at all.

"Put your bathing suit on. I'll wait in the other room."

I grabbed the front of his shirt before he could move away and I laid my cheek against his chest. His arms came up around me and he expelled a long puff of air as he settled his chin on the top of my head. "You make it really hard to walk out of this room."

"I didn't ask you to leave."

He groaned. "Trust me, the thought of burying myself deep inside you is going to haunt me the rest of the day. But if I sleep with you now, you will always wonder if it's the only thing I wanted from you."

"Is it?"

He lifted my head off his chest and pinned me with his dark molten stare. "At first, maybe. But then I spent five minutes with you and in those five minutes I realized you weren't just a warm body… you weren't just the kind of girl I could get out of my system with a fling. I'm not really sure what any of that means… but I do know I'm not going to fuck this up by sleeping with you too fast."

And that's how he claimed the first piece of my heart.

*   *   *

We drove to the beach with the top down on his Mustang. The air was warm, but the moving wind was slightly chilly. But I didn't mind. It was a nice contrast to the warm cup of coffee Cam handed me the minute I came out of the bedroom dressed in a hot-pink bikini and a strapless, black cotton cover-up.

I didn't bother to do my hair. Instead, I just pulled it back into a ponytail with a simple black band and slipped a pair of wide-rimmed black sunglasses on top of my head.

Thanks to our impromptu make out session, I was more awake than usual, but I was still practically a zombie. He chuckled when I clutched the coffee like a lifeline, and he guided me out the door while I thrust my keys at him so he could lock up behind us.

I don't think I'd ever been to the beach at such an early hour. It was stunningly beautiful, with the sky a little overcast and nothing but the sound of the surf in the quiet morning air. It seemed like we were the only two people on this long stretch of empty sand, like everyone else knew we were going to be here and we wanted to be alone.

I sat down and pushed my toes deep into the sand and stared out at the morning waves, spying a shrimping boat off in the distance. Cam laid down his board and then took up the space beside me. I leaned my head on his shoulder and we sat there quietly as the waves lapped at the shore and the breeze swirled around our bodies.

"You do this every morning?"

"Every single day."

"Have you lived here all your life?"

"Yep. Born and raised. My mom says I have salt water in my veins."

I smiled. "Did you make your board?" I said, gesturing to the large surfboard beside him.

"Yeah." He pulled it around and I pulled my legs in closer to my chest to make room. I didn't know much about surfboards, but I did know this one was beautiful. It was fairly long and wide and I figured it was because Cam was at least six feet tall. It was shaped like every other surfboard I'd seen, coming to a sort of point at the top.

The board itself was white, but it had this beautiful sea-green design across it, kind of like a scroll but a little more intricate. The design was heavier at the bottom end and then spread out more as it reached the top of the board. At the very top there was nothing but the white background. Written amongst the scroll design down across the bottom were two words:

Pura Vida

"What does that mean?" I asked him, tracing over the letters with my finger.

"Live purely. It's a popular saying in Costa Rica."

"It's beautiful."

He nodded. "Kind of embodies the way I try to live."

"The whole surfer dude attitude, huh?"

He chuckled. "Yeah, maybe."

"Hmm, I sense a story."

"No story, not really. My parents fought a lot when I was growing up. Never really in front of me, but when they thought I couldn't see. Kids always see that kind of stuff, even when they aren't looking, you know?"

I nodded and rested my head against his shoulder as he spoke.

"Eventually they got divorced, and both of them were so much happier, so much nicer to everyone around them. It taught me that people shouldn't make life so hard. If they aren't happy, they should change it. They should do what makes them happy. We only get so long in life, why spend any of that time being with people who are bad for you or doing things you don't really want to do?"

"How old are you?" I asked, thinking he sounded pretty wise for someone that looked so young.

"Twenty-three."

"No college?"

"School isn't really my thing."

"Art is though," I said, reaching out once more to finger the design on his board. "You painted this design, didn't you?"

"Yeah."

"So you surf by day and bartend by night."

"Sometimes I give surf lessons and I've made a couple custom boards and done some artwork for some friends. Bartending at night just frees up my days, and the money is pretty good so I can save up for that surf and board shop I was telling you about."

"The view's not bad either, right?"

He laughed. "Yeah, the view doesn't hurt."

"Have you ever dated a stripper?" When I took the job at the Mad Hatter I never thought about what other people would think, probably because I hadn't planned on telling anyone. I certainly hadn't thought about what a guy would think—a guy that I might want to date. *Date.* Did I want to date Cam?

Oh yeah.

I got this uneasy feeling, not because I wanted to date him, but because I thought he might not see me as relationship material because I took my clothes off for other men. How could he respect someone like that? How could he be okay with it?

"Define date," he replied, giving me an ornery grin.

I sat up and gave his shoulder a shove. "Spent any time with one with clothes on."

"Then, no, I don't think I've dated a stripper."

I nodded, my suspicions confirmed. I guess I couldn't really blame him. I probably wouldn't get in line to date a stripper either. Heat flooded my cheeks when I thought about earlier this morning. I'd certainly enjoyed his hands and mouth all over me. He probably thought I was some loose floozy who had sex all the time and took off her clothes for everyone.

"Hey," he said. "Where'd you go?"

"Nowhere. I'm still here."

His eyes narrowed on my face. "You know just because I haven't dated a stripper doesn't mean I *wouldn't*."

I didn't answer because it seemed like every answer I could give would be the wrong one. If I said "good," then that would imply that I was trying to date him. And seeing as how we just met, he might think I'm some crazy stalker. But if I told him my real thoughts, about how strippers might not be good girlfriend material, I would basically be insulting myself (not to mention Roxie and all the other girls at the club).

"So you actually going to get on this thing?" he asked, patting the surfboard.

"Well, I do owe you."

He flashed a grin and stood, reaching for my hand to pull me up with him. He used one hand to pull off his T-shirt and toss it into the sand next to my bag. He eyed my cover-up so I slid it off, letting it fall around my ankles and then kicking it over beside his shirt.

"Day-um," he said, a low whistle slipping between his teeth.

The desire from earlier that still swirled inside me threatened to overtake me like a really strong tidal wave, and I did my best to ignore it as his eyes perused every single curve of my body. I adjusted the string bikini bottoms and then the top. The string around my neck had loosened and I turned my back to him and pointed to the string at the back of my neck. "Can you tie this a little tighter?"

His warm fingers felt like a soft caress to the back of my neck and I resisted the urge to shudder. Geez, he was going to think I was a nympho if I kept reacting like this every time he touched me. He worked awfully slow, untying the top completely, adjusting the strings, and then retying them snuggly at the base of my neck.

"How am I supposed to forget about this morning when you're wearing the sexiest bikini I've ever seen?" he whispered into my ear from behind.

"Want me to put on your shirt?"

"Hell no. The thought of all this," he said, running his hands across my shoulders and then down my sides to play with the ties at my hips, "rubbing against my shirt could quite possibly send me over the edge."

"I have a cure for that," I said, turning and smiling at him ruefully. I grabbed his hand and tugged him a few feet toward the water just as a swell rushed up and splashed over our feet and up our calves.

"It's cold!" I squealed.

"It's not that bad," he scoffed.

"So you're a morning person *and* you like cold showers?" I said, making an appalled face. "We can't hang out. You're like an alien to me."

He grabbed me around the waist and tossed me over his shoulder, wading farther into the waves. I pounded on his back with my fists, demanding he put me down.

"You asked for it," he called over the sound of crashing water.

I started to protest, but it was too late.

He dumped me into the surf.

I slipped under as the chilly salt water closed around me. I started to stand and a wave chose that moment to pummel me, knocking me off my feet and tossing me around in the churning dark water.

Strong arms wound around my waist and towed me up, pulling me against his chest. I sputtered, wiping the water from my eyes and pushing my saturated hair out of my face.

"Harlow, are you okay? I didn't mean to scare you," he said, the concern in his voice genuine. Another wave crashed over us and his arms tightened around me and he turned so it broke into his back and his body shielded me from the worst of it.

"Harlow?" he said again once the waves calmed.

I pushed back and looked up, hiding my grin. He was watching me warily, probably wondering if I was going to dissolve into tears.

I launched myself at him, a cry slipping from my lips. I leapt, wrapping my legs around his waist as he caught me, but he wasn't ready for my weight and we both toppled over into the water. We both surfaced several seconds later, both of us still sitting on the sandy floor and laughing.

Our little water war lasted for a while, both of us splashing and leaping at the other. When we tired of the game, we let the waves carry us to shore and I waited while he grabbed his board and brought it out to the water.

"First rule of surfing," he instructed. "Don't fall off."

"Ha. Ha." I said. "Something tells me it won't be that easy."

He launched into a really thorough but entertaining breakdown of the basics of surfing. Before I knew it, he had me on the board and I was learning how to balance and stand. It wasn't easy, staying on a very buoyant moving object in choppy water took a lot of muscle tone that I unfortunately didn't possess.

As we played, the tide began to come in, the waves getting just a little bit rougher. After a mouthful of awful-tasting water, I sat on the sand bar that had formed in the water and told him to show me his moves.

He didn't hesitate and grabbed up the board, wading farther out into the deeper water to catch a wave. I couldn't help but admire the way he looked with his waterlogged board shorts hanging low on his hips, plastered to his butt and thighs, and his broad shoulders glistening under the rising morning sun as droplets of water trailed down over his corded muscles.

He knew the water. He understood the waves. He moved so confidently and assuredly I could have called him the water whisperer. He was so in tune with the surf that he seemed to understand exactly how each wave would crest and how to follow it expertly.

Suddenly, getting up at six a.m. seemed like the best thing I'd ever done.

After catching a few waves, he slid to a stop beside me. "Want to give it one more shot?"

"Sure," I said, and he wrapped his hand around mine, keeping hold of it while we jumped over waves.

I could get used to this.

Early morning kisses, coffee on the beach, playing in the sun and the sand. Cam was definitely on to something with the whole "Pura Vida" thing. Of course, none of this would have been as much fun if he wasn't with me.

"Looks like a good one's coming in," he said, pointing out into the distance where a wave was just beginning to form.

He positioned the board and me, repeating what to do one more time as the wave traveled closer. Then he was yelling for me to go, to catch the wave.

His passion was catching and so I went, concentrating on everything he showed me, wanting to make him proud.

And then I jumped up on the board, my legs wobbly and threatening to collapse as cool sea air sprayed my skin. I was afraid I might fall, but I held firm as I coasted along with the wave. I smiled. It was incredible.

Behind me, Cam let out a great whoop and I turned to smile at him.

That was my mistake.

I stopped concentrating. I wasn't paying attention. Well, I was paying attention, just not to what I was doing.

The surfboard crashed into the sand bar where I'd just been sitting and I went flying, plunging into the churning, dark waves.

8

Washed up. That's exactly how I felt in the moment. The waves were punishing, tumbling over me every single time I thought I found my footing. The sand beneath me would feel like concrete in one moment; then the next it would give way like a sink hole and suck me farther into the water.

I flailed my arms about, trying to swim toward the surface, trying to break free, but because of the way I was being pounded, I began to lose which way was up.

I opened my eyes, trying to discern the direction, but all I could see was cloudy water that would suddenly turn white when a new wave crashed around me. I fought hard, twisting and turning, holding off the panic that sank into me like a set of icy, sharp claws.

When I finally managed to break the surface and gasp for air, I was punished by yet another huge swell of water that shoved me back under with the force of a bulldozer.

And then my legs were somehow above my head and I was sinking, sinking until the back of my head struck something so unforgiving that my struggling ceased.

Even though I stopped moving, my body did not. It was still being tugged at by the very greedy sea.

Finally I settled, sinking to the hard-packed sand where I rested my cheek against the warmth.

The water hadn't been this warm moments ago.

The sand didn't feel quite as gritty as it usually did.

And the sound… the sound of the waves seemed farther away.

"Breathe, damn it!" someone yelled. "*Breathe!*"

I began to cough—my throat making these retching gurgling sounds—and then water began to ooze out of my mouth. I was thrust onto my side as the water continued to come up and I continued to cough.

When the water was gone, oxygen arrived. It filled my lungs completely. What was once empty was now overfull. I gasped in great breaths, relief pouring through my body and making me sink back onto the ground.

"Harlow," a voice said.

It was a really good voice and my body rolled toward it.

"Baby, open your eyes."

I did, blinking away the water that made my vision blurry and squinting against the sun peeking through a cloud.

"Cam?" I said. The back of my throat burned and so did my nose.

His face was pale, his hair plastered to his forehead, and he was hunching forward over me like I needed some kind of shield.

I almost drowned.

I groaned. "There went my surfer of the year award," I whined.

His laugh was strained as his arms encircled me and dragged my sand-crusted body into his lap. "I think you just took about ten years off my life."

"I'm sorry."

"This isn't your fault," he said, stroking my cheek. "I should never have set you loose on that wave. The water was getting too rough."

"I had a good time," I protested, trying to sit up. Pain shot through my head. "Until I hit my head."

"You hit your head?" he said frantically as his fingers sank into my hair.

I yelped.

"Fuck," he swore. "I didn't mean to hurt you."

"If it wasn't for you, I'd be shark bait right about now."

I felt a faint shudder move through his limbs when they tightened around me. "I tried to get there sooner. The current grabbed you and pulled you away."

"It's okay."

"No, it isn't," he said, his voice hard. He slipped his arm under my shoulders. "Can you sit up? I need to check your head."

I did and then lifted my fingers to where my skull throbbed.

Cam brushed away my fingers and then gently probed the area I pointed out. "You're not bleeding, thank God," he announced. "But you have a knot the size of a walnut back here."

"I'll live."

"I'm taking you to the hospital."

"I don't need to go to the hospital. I'm fine." Not to mention, I wasn't going spend all the money I just made on a doctor bill.

"You could have a concussion."

"I don't."

"Does anything else hurt?"

"No."

"Can you stand?"

"If you want me to stand, you have to release the death grip you have on my body."

He released me and stood, gingerly helping me to my feet. I really didn't feel that bad, just a little dizzy and very water logged. He put his arm around my waist and supported some of my weight as we walked over toward our stuff.

"Wonder what time it is?" I said and bent to retrieve my cell phone from my bag. Bending over wasn't a good idea, as all the blood rushed to my head way to fast and I swayed.

"Whoa," Cam said, pulling me back up. Then his mouth pulled into a grim line. "We're going to the doctor."

"I have to work at ten," I protested.

"Call in and tell them you can't make it."

"I can't do that! I might get fired."

"They aren't going to fire you for having a head injury."

"I can't miss work." I worried, thinking about the money I'd be losing.

Cam pretty much ignored me and grabbed up my cover-up and then gently pulled it over my head. I lifted my arms and he pulled it down, adjusting it so it covered my bikini.

"Sit down for a second. I'm going to go grab my board down by the water. Then we'll go."

It felt good to sit down. My body was so incredibly tired. I suddenly felt like I'd just spent ten rounds in a boxing ring and I lost every single one of them.

Cam returned, tossed on his shirt, and grabbed up my bag and his board. "Wait here," he said as he jogged it all toward the car.

I got up, brushing away what I could of the sand and followed after him. I made it about twenty feet when everything kind of tilted on me. I stopped walking and just focused on the ground, pushing away the worst of the dizziness.

Cam appeared, slowly picking me up and carrying me to the Mustang. I wasn't about to complain because he was touching me and I loved when he touched me.

He didn't say anything as he sat me in the passenger seat and buckled the seat belt around my body. Before he pulled away, he pressed a tender kiss on my lips.

"What was that for?" I asked.

"It wasn't for you. It was for me."

Well, if that wasn't just the most perfect thing he could say. Like ever.

I pretty much replayed those words in my head until he pulled into the parking lot of some kind of medical clinic. "We don't need to be here."

"Humor me."

I sighed. And gave in. There wasn't one woman on this earth that still had ovaries that wouldn't have given in to his pleading, concerned stare.

Before going inside, I called my boss and explained that I fell and hit my head and was currently at the doctor being looked at for a concussion (I certainly wasn't going to tell him that I was out surfing before work). I thought he would be angry about it being only an hour before my shift started, but he was very understanding and asked me to bring in a doctor's slip clearing me for work and being out in the heat when I came to work next.

"Well, at least now I can be home to help Roxie move in," I said as we walked through the parking lot.

"Roxie's moving in with you?"

"Yeah. She kicked her cheating boyfriend to the curb and I needed a roommate to help cover rent."

"Wonder what Adam will say about her newly single status?"

"Why would Adam care?" I asked, watching him out of the corner of my eye.

"I see the way he sometimes looks at her."

"Probably the same way she looks at him."

He opened the door to the clinic and ushered me inside, depositing me in a chair and then insisting on checking me in. I settled into the seat and got ready for a wait. All these clinics had a wait. It was the most annoying thing ever.

My phone started ringing, the sound partially muffled from inside my bag. I pulled it out just as Cam was sitting down in the chair right beside mine. The phone rang again and I glanced at the screen and groaned.

It was my mother.

Third time she tried to call this week.

I shut off the ringer and stuffed it back into my bag, promising myself I would call her back after we left the doctor.

"Didn't feel like talking?" Cam asked, casually draping his arm across the back of my chair. I leaned toward him. The air-conditioner in here was set to arctic.

"It was my mother," I said, like that explained it all.

"You two don't get along?"

"Actually, we do. But my mother has very clear ideas about how she thinks I should be living my life. Being here isn't really one of them."

He arched a brow. "She didn't want you to go to college?"

"Maybe community college or a technical school in Beaufort. But moving to Myrtle Beach to study psychology? She didn't approve."

"She give a reason?"

"I think she just wanted me close by where she could give an opinion on every aspect of my life. She wanted me to work at a bank, settle down, and get married. Be like her. There isn't anything wrong with that. It just isn't what I wanted."

"Seems like you have a little *Pura Vida* of your own." The way he said those two words… they flowed silkily with a slight roll of his tongue. I leaned into his side just a little closer.

The nurse came out of the side door at the front of the waiting room and called my name. I should have known. The one time I actually didn't mind sitting around and waiting was the one time they called me right back.

Cam stood when I did and I gave him a surprised look. "I'm going with you," he said in a voice that left no room for argument.

His palm fitted itself against the small of my back as we both followed the nurse into a tiny room with a table covered in that white noisy paper. She took some vitals and asked some questions and then exited the room, leaving us to wait for the doctor.

The knot on the back of my head was tender and I investigated the area around it with my fingers. Cam noticed and pulled my hand away. "Don't irritate it."

You'd think I was beating myself in the head with something. "It hurts." I complained.

"I should have known better than to take a klutz like you surfing."

I scowled.

"Let me see," he said softly, coming closer to nudge his hips between my knees and taking my head in his hands. He titled it down and parted the still damp hair away from the sore area.

"What the hell did you hit your head on?" he murmured, brushing his fingers ever so lightly over the raised bump.

"The ground?" I guessed.

"I'm sorry, babe," he murmured, tilting my head back up and pressing a kiss to the corner of my lips.

If he kept touching me, I was going to find some other way to hurt myself just so he would keep doing it.

There was a rap on the door and Cam pulled away as a doctor in a white coat came in holding a piece of paper. "You hit your head?" he asked, looking up at me.

"I was surfing and I fell. I'm not sure what I hit my head on. The water was too dark for me to see."

"Did you lose consciousness?"

I thought about how I thought I'd been lying on the bottom of the ocean when really I had been against Cam's chest. "No, but I was disoriented at first."

"Headache?"

"Yes."

"Nausea?"

"Not really."

The questions continued as he checked my eyes, the bump on my head, and finally he stepped back.

"I would say you likely have a mild concussion."

"What does that mean?" Cam asked.

"Just means you're going to have a headache for a day or two. Since it's mild, some over-the-counter pain relievers will probably be enough for the pain. No driving for a day or two. If you feel any new symptoms, come back here immediately. If the swelling on your head isn't gone in a few days, come back in. Do not go to sleep for at least two hours. When you do go to sleep, have someone wake you every couple hours just to be sure you're all right."

"All that for a bump on the head?" I asked, feeling slightly put out.

He smiled. "I would say it could have been far worse. At least you weren't alone and he was able to pull you out of the water."

The doctor handed me a couple papers and told us we were free to go.

I shoved the papers in my bag and braced myself to jump off the tall table. But Cam appeared, gripping my waist and gently setting me on my feet. Without saying a word, he wrapped his fingers around mine and walked us through the office.

When I tried to steer myself toward the reception counter, he pulled me the other way. "I have to check out, Cam. I need to pay the bill."

"I already paid."

I felt my eyes grow wide. "What! Why would you do that?"

"Because that bump on your head is my fault."

"No, it's not."

"You were on my surfboard."

"Cam, I'm a grown woman. I'm not your responsibility."

"I'm taking care of you today."

"You are?"

"Yes, so don't even try to get rid of me."

An entire day with Cam?

Suddenly, almost drowning and having a concussion seemed like a massive stroke of luck.

9

It was well after ten when Cam parked the Mustang in the lot of my apartment building. This building wasn't nearly as tall as his. It looked more Spanish style, with a terracotta tiled roof, a pale-yellow stucco exterior, and was longer than it was tall. It was only two stories high with steps running between each of the units. My unit was on the second floor in the center of the building.

"Roxie's here," I said, glancing up to see the door to the apartment open with boxes piled just outside the door. "Looks like she's already moving in."

"Hey!" I called, stepping around the boxes and going inside.

Roxie poked her head out of her new bedroom. "Violet! I thought you had to work."

"She hit her head," Cam explained. (And just like a typical guy, he only said enough to make it sound far worse than it was).

"Oh my God! What happened?" She rushed to my side, looking me over. I gave her a more thorough explanation and then sat on the sofa.

"A couple Motrin and I'll be fine."

Roxie hit Cam in the stomach with her fist. "Jerk!"

"Want me to help carry in some boxes?"

"I love you!" she exclaimed, flinging her arms around him.

I laughed.

"I do all the heavy lifting and he gets a hug?" someone grumbled from behind a stack of boxes in the doorway.

When he carried them around the couch, I saw that it was Adam as he disappeared into her room. I gave her an *oh my gosh!* look and she actually blushed.

Before I could get the scoop, Adam came back into the living room. "Good, someone with actual muscles," he said, looking at Cam. "Can you give me a hand with her mattress?"

When they were gone, I motioned for Roxie to sit next to me. "So… Adam's helping you move?"

She nodded. "When I asked him if I could leave last night to look at your place, he offered to use his truck to move me in today."

"Wow. Talk about a boss who cares about his employees."

"I told you we're friends," she said. Then she added, "He's been after me for a while to get rid of Craig."

"He has?" I leaned closer, sensing a story.

"He caught me crying in the ladies' room one day during work and forced the reason out of me. That was the first time I caught him cheating."

"Sounds like he's very protective."

"I think he's just glad he won't find me crying in the bathroom anymore." She grinned ruefully. Today she was wearing a pair of cut-off shorts and a black tank top, which accentuated her tiny waist and the way her hips flared out provocatively.

I wouldn't be surprised at all if Adam was interested in her. "Cam thinks Adam likes you."

Her eyes got wide as saucers. "He does?"

I grinned and nodded.

Her smile slipped. "Well, he won't date any of his dancers so it doesn't matter."

I didn't say anything else because the guys appeared hauling a large white mattress. After that, we all worked together helping her get all her stuff out of Adam's truck and into the apartment.

Correction: they all unloaded Adam's truck and I sat around unpacking boxes (mostly clothes) because Cam wouldn't let me carry anything.

When Adam heard about my concussion, he almost forced me to stay home from work that night, but I flat out refused. There was no way I was going to miss work. I needed the money.

Cam wasn't happy, but that was just too bad.

He also wasn't very happy when he had to leave me in the care of Roxie so he could go home and get ready for work.

I really wanted to take a nap, but I knew if I did, Roxie would be checking on me every five seconds and getting up for work would be a pain so I took a shower instead.

The cool water felt good as it washed away what was left of the sand and the sea from the morning. I washed my hair gently, wincing when the spray came into contact with the bump. After that, I distracted myself with thoughts of Cam and me in my bed this morning.

Kissing him was like the first bite of really fattening ice cream. Like lying in bed and listening to the sound of a thunderstorm or being a kid on Christmas Eve. Sinful, comfortable, but thoroughly exciting.

He stirred up so many different emotions in me at the exact same time it was a little frightening. But not necessarily in a bad way. I'd never met anyone like him before. Someone who was casual but knew what they wanted out of life. It's like he knew exactly where he was going, but he wasn't in a hurry. He didn't drive himself crazy trying to get to the end goal of his plan.

I liked that.

The way he looked certainly didn't hurt anything either. My God, his body was the total package. Lean but cut, tan, and smooth. He moved with the grace of an athlete (surfing does a body good) and he smiled like a guy with some kind of naughty secret.

And that dimple… I wanted to lick it.

I'd never felt so attracted to a guy. I'd never felt the kind of sexual charge that coursed through my body whenever he was around. It was so strong that I knew if he hadn't stopped things this morning, I would have slept with him. I wouldn't be a virgin anymore.

He said he didn't want to rush things, but my body didn't care about how fast we moved. My body felt like it had been waiting an entire lifetime for someone to make me feel like this.

What about my head? My heart?

My head told me waiting wasn't a bad thing. My head told me every girl should be cautious.

And my heart… my heart whispered that he could be the one. It told me I wasn't in love with him, not yet, but it was only a matter of time.

If Cam had only wanted one thing from me, his actions would have told me so. Yes, he would have driven me to the medical center; he might even have stayed. But he wouldn't have followed me back into the exam room. He wouldn't have paid the bill. And as silly as it was… my mind kept picturing that heart he drew on my cup of lemonade.

It appeared that my heart and my body was ganging up against my brain and trying to overthrow it.

After my shower, I pulled on a white T-shirt dress, thinking it would show off the little bit of tan I got this morning at the beach. I dried my hair into a smooth, straight style and then curled the pieces around my face to feather out over my shoulders.

When I was putting on my makeup, someone rang the doorbell. I peeked out of my bedroom and glanced toward Roxie's room. Her door pulled open and she stuck her head out. "You expecting someone?" she asked.

"No. Are you?"

Roxie shook her head and bit her lower lip. "Do you think he followed me?"

"Who?"

"Craig."

Unease slithered through me. "Was he mad you moved out?"

She nodded.

Judging from the look on her face, I wondered if he did more to her than cheat. "Go back in your room," I told her, walking toward the door.

If it were Craig, I would lie and tell him he had the wrong apartment. Times like this, I wish I had one of those peephole things in the door.

"Who is it?" I called out, deciding I was too chicken to open it and see.

"It's Cam."

I let out a relieved breath and pulled open the door. "Hey, sorry about that."

"What's the matter?" he said, his eyes narrowing on my face as he walked inside.

"Nothing."

Roxie opened her door and looked out, the relief on her face plain.

Cam looked at me with a lifted brow. "Nothing?"

"We thought it might be Craig," Roxie explained.

His lips thinned. "Does he know where you are?"

"I didn't tell him."

"What are you doing here?" I asked, trying to change the subject.

"I came to drive you to work. You can't drive, remember?"

I didn't bother to point out that Roxie and I both worked tonight and at the same place.

"How's your head?" he asked, running those onyx-colored eyes over me.

"It's good. I'm just going to grab my stuff. I'll be out in a sec."

I turned back toward my room and ignored Roxie who was watching us intently from her bedroom door. If she teased me about Cam later, I would tease her about Adam.

In my room, I finished up my makeup, sprayed my hair with hairspray, and grabbed my duffel, which was still packed from the night before. On my way out of the bedroom, I picked up my phone and remembered I forgot to call my mother back.

I hit her name in the contacts and the phone started ringing. I had to admit, I felt a little relieved when her voicemail came over the line.

"This is Veronica. Leave a message."

Beep.

"Hey, Mom, sorry I missed your call earlier today. I'm heading into work now, but I will call you in the morning and we can catch up. Tell Daddy I said hi!"

Then I disconnected the line and shoved the phone in my bag.

"You ready?" Cam said from just behind me.

I jumped, putting a hand to my chest. "You snuck up on me!"

"You were on the phone. I was trying to be quiet." His eyes sparked with mischief.

"You know Roxie could have taken me to work."

His eyes darkened. "Is her ex some kind of threat?"

I wrinkled my nose. "I don't know. I didn't think so..."

"But when I knocked on the door, she got scared."

I nodded. "I knew he was a dirt bag, cheated on her and stuff, but she never said anything about him hurting her physically."

"Think she would tell you?"

I thought that over. "Maybe not. We haven't known each other that long."

"Maybe she shouldn't live here."

"Shh!" I shushed him, my eyes flying to the door. "I am not kicking her out!"

"It might not be safe."

"I'm perfectly safe. Our doors lock and this apartment is on the second floor." I crossed my arms over my chest. "Besides, where else is she supposed to go? And I like her."

"I like her, too."

"She already signed the lease anyway," I finished, grabbing my duffle. This conversation was over.

"Hey," Cam said when I would have brushed past him. His hand wrapped around my upper arm and towed me closer. "Don't be mad. I'm just thinking about your safety."

"And I appreciate it, but I'm fine."

He reached out and slid the duffle strap off my shoulder and hefted it onto his. Then his hand moved off of my arm and slid around my back, pulling me closer so my body came directly up against him.

He dipped his head and captured my lips as his other arm wound around me, locking me in place. A low groan rumbled in the back of his throat as our lips collided over and over. I reached up, my hands sliding around his head and burying themselves in his hair at the base of his neck. I tugged at the strands, drawing him closer, and my tongue snaked out to mingle with his.

His hands didn't stay at my back for very long. Instead, they cupped my butt, pressing me even closer, and I gasped when his solid arousal brushed against my belly. Lust, plain and simple, swamped me. If it had been an ocean, I surely would have drowned. It was like I was made just for him and he knew exactly how to illicit desires, cravings, needs from me that I was beginning to think I didn't possess.

I delved my hands into the neck of his shirt, my fingernails raking over the smooth skin of his upper back. His shirt was in my way. I didn't want it between us. I wanted to run my hands all over the body I couldn't stop staring at this morning on the beach.

But he pulled away. "Fuck, Harlow. You're so damn responsive. Every time I touch you, it's like you melt in my palms."

I totally did.

It was completely embarrassing.

Once again, Harlow acts like a nympho.

"I'm sorry," I apologized, then paused. What did a girl say when she acted like a complete ho? I don't get out much? Yeah, because that would be believable. Hell, at this point I was starting to think I lost my virginity along the way and just forgot.

Sex with Cam would be unforgettable.

Ahh, geez. There I go again.

Maybe I *was* a nympho.

"Don't ever apologize," he said, pulling me against him and kissing the top of my head. "I fucking love it. You make me feel like I have some kinda sex powers."

I laughed.

"Are you laughing at me?" he growled.

"Only a guy would think he has sex powers."

"You saying I don't?" he asked slyly, reaching down and slipping his fingers up my dress and caressing my inner thighs.

My back arched and I sucked in a breath.

He chuckled. "Yep. I got powers."

Then he released me and hitched my bag a little farther onto his shoulder. "C'mon, we're going to be late."

I called a good-bye to Roxie and we headed down to the curb. "No bike?" I said, a little disappointed.

"I didn't think a helmet would feel too good over that knot on your head. Besides, you have a concussion. Traveling on a bike isn't a good idea."

"You act like I need to be on bed rest," I said, rolling my eyes.

"Would bed rest really be that bad?" he asked, giving me a heated stare.

My cheeks flushed.

He laughed.

"You're quite the contradiction, babe. One minute you're like a firecracker in my arms and the next minute, you're blushing like a virgin."

A nervous laugh slipped out as I reached for the door and slid into the passenger seat. He caught the door as I swung it closed. He looked at me with squinty eyes. I could see the debate raging inside his head... was she or wasn't she?

I licked my lips nervously, not really sure what to say.

"Harlow," he said, his voice strangely hoarse.

My eyes met his.

"Shit," he swore. He knelt down between the door and my seat. "Are you a virgin?" he whispered.

"Yeah."

He groaned... the kind of groan that implied pain. "I'm sorry."

"Why are you sorry?"

"Because of this morning… in bed. I went too far. I just… the way you respond to me, I would have sworn you were experienced."

My cheeks flamed. This wasn't exactly the kind of conversation I wanted to have. But if I wasn't mature enough to have this conversation with him, then I had no business being in his arms. And I wholly wanted to be in his arms.

"You didn't go too far. I… wanted it, which you could tell." I took a deep breath. "I've never felt like this, *like that*, with anyone before."

"Yeah, well, I haven't either. And I'm not a virgin."

"Really?"

He rubbed a hand over his jaw. "No, that ship sailed a long time ago."

I rolled my eyes. "I meant that you haven't felt like this before either."

He stood and shut the door between us but was able to lean over the side because the top was still down. Balancing on the top of the door, he leaned close, kissing me in a way that was meant to be brief but deepened the minute our lips moved.

"Yeah," he said, pulling back and motioning between us. "This is new even for me."

I tilted my head to the side. "So we're kind of both virgins?"

"I wouldn't go that far, babe." He chuckled and kissed me on the tip of my nose. Then he went around and jumped into the car without opening his door.

Before backing out of the parking spot, he looked at me and half smiled. "A stripper who's a virgin. That's got to be a first."

The wind carried away my laugh as we drove
away.

10

The Mad Hatter was beyond packed. It was so busy that every table was full. There were two bachelor parties on both sides of the room, and it was standing room only around the stage.

It made me incredibly nervous.

"Is every weekend like this?" I asked Roxie as we dressed backstage.

"Pretty much."

My stomach churned. I felt like I was going to be sick. How in the world was I going to convince a crowd this big that I was sexy without taking off my clothes?

The first three girls that just finished their routines stripped all the way down to nothing but thongs. Money practically rained down on them as they danced.

I wasn't sure I could do that, even for raining money.

I missed my first two dances of the night because the bar was so packed that Adam told me to stay on the floor and serve drinks. I didn't mind; in fact, I was relieved. I put on the black bustier, the stockings, and the heels and laughed and smiled with the best of them. I made pretty good tips and at least doing this, I felt a little less exposed.

But as the night went on, the crowd grew louder and drunker.

Adam found me and told me to get backstage so I could do some dancing to give some of the other girls a break.

"Don't freak out," Roxie told me over the music and the crowd.

I pulled out a pink bustier, one that laced up the front with black satin ribbons. Then I put on a tiny pair of black boy shorts with pink skulls on them. The purple stripe was already in my hair and I decided just to leave it down around my shoulders. Then I slipped on the black stilettos and added some pink lipstick and some extra eye makeup.

"That outfit is hot," Roxie said, looking me over.

"I hope so," I muttered.

I went to my place behind the curtain as my heart pounded and my palms sweated. The crowd was so loud that I had to strain to hear the DJ announce me.

The music started up (another classic rock song), and I started moving, stepping out and strutting down the stage toward the pole. I'd avoided the pole so far, but I didn't know what else to do.

As I strutted, my shoe caught on something (likely thin air) and I stumbled. Thankfully, I didn't fall, but one of the guys pushed up to the edge of the stage reached out and grabbed my waist. "Whoa there, sweetheart," he said, pushing me back up and slapping me on the butt.

I glanced toward the back of the club where Ty stood glaring in the direction of mister grabby hands. I gave him a slight shake of my head and he relaxed. Then I turned back to the man who touched me and put the toe of my heel on his shoulder. The crowd liked that so I did a little move and then shoved off the guy, making him fall backward.

He deserved it.

Hands reached for me as I turned myself around the pole, and I wanted to gag. I did not want just anyone's hands on me. I only wanted one set of hands on me.

Cam's.

Just thinking his name was a mistake because it halted my movements, and I turned in the direction of the bar, my eyes automatically seeking him out.

He was handing someone a beer when he seemed to sense I was looking and he glanced up. Our eyes met.

He nodded his head ever so slightly, telling me I could do this.

I started moving.

For him.

I pretended he was the only guy in the room.

In that moment, he was.

I stuck a finger in my mouth, wet it, and then trailed it down my chest. My fingers scraped all the way down my thighs and then back up, right into the center of my legs. Cam's eyes never left me as he leaned forward on the bar, still watching.

I spun around, spreading my legs and then grabbing my butt with both hands. I stopped and looked over my shoulder, directly at him.

And then I strutted to the end of the stage where two men were standing, watching. "Give a girl a hand, boys?" I said, holding out my hands.

They were only too happy to oblige and then both lifted me down.

The crowd parted as I moved; the spotlight followed the path I took. My eyes never strayed from my target, from my destination.

When I got to the bar, I grabbed a man by the back of his shirt (frankly, I was offended he wasn't looking at me to begin with) and tugged, yanking him away from the bar.

"Hey!" he yelled until he got an eyeful.

I smiled, grabbed his bottle of beer, and took a long pull. The crowd cheered. Then I handed it to him and he held it up like he won some award. Placing both palms on the top of the bar, I hoisted myself up (I only slipped a little) and sat on the bar, my legs dangling over the side.

Cam was a little farther down so I crawled, my movements long and drawn out, down the bar toward him. I felt the boy shorts ride up my butt, but I didn't fix them… I didn't care.

He stood up straighter, making room as I got closer. Beside him there was a little holder full of plastic test tubes that were half full of electric-blue shots. I had no clue what kind of alcohol was in them. It didn't matter.

I hoped, I prayed that Cam played into this because he was about to become part of my routine. If he didn't cooperate, I was pretty sure I would have to hide in the bathroom the rest of the night.

I stood directly over him, giving him a full-on view of my backside, and then leaned down and picked up one of the test tubes. I lifted it high so everyone could see.

Then I slid the tube right down between my breasts.

I heard the whistling, the catcalls, but I blocked them out. I looked at Cam and sank to my knees right there on the bar, sticking my chest near his face.

I curled my hand around the nape of his neck, just below the black fedora perched on his head, and drew him closer. I felt a laugh rumble through him and I had a momentary freak-out thinking he was going to pull away.

But he didn't.

His lips went searching for the tube. The spotlight was hot as it highlighted us and his lips were cool as they slid over my cleavage and found the tube. He yanked it up with his teeth, then tipped his head back and drained the liquid.

The crowd was in a good frenzy now as I stood and strutted down the bar. I crooked my finger at Cam, hoping he would follow, and thankfully, he did.

I reached for the black silk ribbon lacing up the corset and I pulled, slowly untying the garment. I started low near my belly button and pulled the ribbon until the corset was completely open all the way up to just beneath my breasts.

I glanced at Cam.

I was out of ideas.

But he wasn't.

He grabbed an empty shot glass off the bar and held it up. The men cheered (I had no idea why) and then he flung it up, flipping it in midair, and caught it. Then he slammed it down on the bar in between my legs and pointed.

I had no idea what that meant.

"Lay down," he mouthed.

I took my time, making a production out of it as I draped myself across the top of the bar. By now my first song was over and the DJ had started another, but the one he picked went perfectly with the mood so I went with it.

When I was lying on the bar with my back arched in a way I prayed was provocative and not stupid, Cam poured a shot of honey-colored liquor into the glass. Then he parted the opening of my corset, completely exposing my midsection.

I wasn't prepared for what he did next.

He licked across my stomach, just above my belly button. His tongue was like a fire blazing a scorching trail across my skin. I didn't have to pretend I liked it.

Because I did.

I liked it so much my back arched even farther off the bar. Then he sprinkled something across the wet path he left on my skin. It was gritty and white. Salt.

Then he held up a wedge of lime and tucked it between my breasts, right where the ribbon was coming loose.

The shot glass was cold when he set it in the center of my stomach. I held my breath, praying I wouldn't move and cause it to spill.

The crowd chanted, "Do it!" and he grinned, licked the salt off my stomach, snatched the shot glass, and slammed back the tequila. Then he dove into my cleavage after the lime, taking a little longer than I thought he really needed and making my nipples harden in the process, before pulling back with the green rind sticking out of his mouth.

Men were high-fiving each other all over the place.

Idiots.

Cam reached over and discreetly tugged my corset together, and then I stood. My eyes locked on a man standing at the edge of the bar against a wall… completely shrouded in shadow.

He was staring at me.

I could feel it.

A shiver worked its way up my spine.

On impulse, I grabbed the fedora off Cam's head and spun it onto mine, tipping it over my face and halting in position. The music cut off. The spotlight went out.

Money flooded the top of the bar.

It was over.

Thank Baby Jesus the routine was over.

And I wasn't naked!

Cam reached for me, lifting me off the bar and sitting me on the side where he was, effectively putting a barrier between me and all the strange, grabby hands. "I so owe you for this," I told him as he helped me gather the money off the bar.

"Are you kidding me?" he whispered in my ear. "That was my pleasure."

Ty appeared at the end of the bar to escort me backstage and I was beyond thankful. As we made our way through the crowd, I got an eerie feeling and I looked over my shoulder toward where I saw the man standing in the shadows.

He was gone.

*   *   *

Roxie was already on stage doing her routine when I made my way to my dressing table. A couple of the girls congratulated me on the dance as I walked by, and I smiled and thanked them when all I really wanted was a moment of quiet.

My cell phone was ringing on top of my dressing table when I approached. It was my mother. Again. Concerned that something was wrong, I answered.

"Mom?" I said, moving toward the back of the room where the community clothes and wigs were. "Is everything okay?"

"Harlow? Where are you? What's all that noise?"

"I got another job, waiting tables. That's the music in the background." Okay, it wasn't a total lie. I did wait tables… in tiny outfits and in between my dances.

"Another job? Are you having money problems, honey?"

She would go straight to that.

"No, Mom, everything is fine." That wasn't a total lie either. I didn't need money. I just scraped a whole bucketful off the bar. "Is there something wrong?"

"I just called — tell — that—" I pressed a finger to my ear to block out some of the noise.

"I can't hear you. You're breaking up," I said.

"— tell you — came—"

I pulled the phone away from my ear. One bar. Practically no reception.

"Mom, are you and Daddy okay?"

"Yes—" I heard her say.

"I'm going to have to call you back in the morning. My reception is really bad in here."

"Wh— Harlow?" And then she was gone. The call dropped.

"Stupid cell phones," I muttered. At least I knew that she and my dad were okay. Everything else could wait 'til morning.

Hopefully she would have forgotten about my new job by then and would forget to ask for the details. My mom loved details.

I forgot completely about the phone call after that because I got so busy waiting tables. The crowd finally began to clear at two a.m. and Adam told me I could go. The only dance I did was the one on the bar.

I wasn't complaining.

I counted out my tips and smiled. Another eight hundred-dollar night. I cashed out all the singles at the bar and then went in the back to exchange the boy shorts and corset for my white T-shirt dress. I used a cleansing wipe to clean off most of the makeup from my face, but I let down my hair.

I was literally exhausted.

The Motrin I took wore off hours ago. My head was pounding and the goose egg on the back of my head hurt.

I just wanted my bed and quiet.

Cam was leaning against the wall by the bathrooms when I exited backstage. He had replaced the black bowtie with a snug white T-shirt and his black leather jacket dangled from his hand.

He pushed off the wall when he saw me, prowling closer, and used his body to push mine back against the door I just exited through.

"You drove me crazy tonight," he murmured, ducking his head and taking my lips hostage. He could kidnap me anytime.

"Those little shorts," he murmured between kisses, "have got to be the sexiest thing"—more kisses—"I have ever seen." More kisses.

I giggled. "Glad you liked them."

He pulled back and swiped the pad of his thumb across my lower lip. "How are you feeling, babe?"

"I've been better."

He held out the jacket and I slipped my arms into it and he tucked it around me. The sleeves fell well past my hands and I smiled. "C'mon. Let's go."

"Adam said you could leave too?"

"He knows I'm your ride."

I breathed a sigh of relief when I finally stepped outside on the pavement. "That place was loud," I muttered as we walked toward the Mustang.

"Head hurt?"

"A little."

We didn't say anything on the short ride to my apartment. When we got there, Cam reached into the back and pulled out a dark-colored backpack.

"What's that for?" I asked curiously.

"I'm staying here tonight."

"You are?" I said, surprised.

"Someone has to wake you up every couple hours."

I groaned. "I'm fine. I've been awake *forever*."

He shook his head. "The doctor said—"

"Fine. You want to stay, stay." I was way too tired to argue.

I watched as he put the ragtop up and locked the doors to the car, and then we both trudged upstairs and into my dark apartment.

I turned on a lamp by the couch and told Cam to make himself at home and then grabbed my PJs and shut myself in the bathroom.

I washed off the rest of my makeup, brushed my teeth, and used some faucet water to swallow another Motrin. Grabbing up my T-shirt dress and undergarments, I switched off the bathroom light and padded into my bedroom, wearing my boxers and tank top.

Cam wasn't in the living room as I crossed through, and I briefly wondered if he was in the kitchen.

He wasn't.

He was lying in my bed.

Without a shirt.

"What are you doing?" I asked him as my desire stole my breath and I forgot all about my headache and how exhausted I was. I'd never seen my bed look so good or so inviting.

"You said to make myself at home."

I laughed and dumped my clothes on the floor. I'd deal with them later. "And you took that as an invite into my bed?"

His grin was slow. "I figured if you needed me, I should be close by."

"Uh-huh," I said, going around to climb into the opposite side. Thank goodness I had a queen-size or there would be no room for me. Not that it mattered. I would find a way to squeeze in beside him even if my bed were the size of a sardine can.

"Nice room you have here."

The walls were painted a light cream color; the headboard was one of those DIY projects my old roommate helped me make and was padded with a chocolate-colored faux-suede material. All the bedding was white, and there were various throw pillows in assorted shades of blue. The dresser and vanity were both painted a robin's egg blue and there was a large framed mirror propped against one of the walls. The only other decorations in here were curtains that were horizontally striped with alternating colors of cream and blue.

"Thanks."

I settled against the pillows, thinking this was the first time I ever had a guy in my bed. He got up and walked toward the door. Somehow I thought when I finally did have a guy in my bed (whether or not he invited himself), he would have stayed a little longer.

He closed the door and then turned and looked at me. "I wouldn't want to wake Roxie every time I wake you up."

"I am not responsible for any bodily harm that comes to you if you actually try to wake me up."

"You wouldn't hurt me."

I snorted.

"Tell me something, Harlow," he said, moving back toward the bed. I barely heard him speak. I was way to entranced by the way his gym shorts hung low, exposing those parallel muscles that cut his hips and disappeared beneath the fabric. "Is this the first time you've had a man in your bed?"

"Yes." If I had been thinking clearly, I would have come up with a less lame response.

"Can't say I'm not happy about that." He pulled the sheet up over us both.

"Thank you for tonight," I said. "At the bar."

"Were you nervous?"

I nodded. "I'm a terrible stripper."

"You're not so bad," he said, sliding lower beneath the covers and turning on his side to face me. A lock of blond hair fell over his forehead and I so badly wanted to push it back. But I felt a little shy all of the sudden. "You just need to relax."

"It's hard to relax in a crowd of drunk, grabby strangers."

"That guy was lucky he let go when he did," he said, his voice turning dark.

"I was kind of relieved when Adam told me to work the floor."

He grinned. "I told him you didn't feel well."

"You did?" I gasped.

He nodded. "You should have seen your face when we turned into the lot and there was nowhere to park."

I groaned and he laughed. "Complete and utter panic."

"I don't know how you deal with all those people."

"Hey, people are always nice to the guy with the beer."

I giggled. He was a really good guy. Almost from the moment we met, he'd been looking out for me, even when I wasn't paying attention (okay, I had a horrible attention span).

I reached out and brushed the hair off his forehead. His eyes closed. Feeling a little bolder, I ran my hand through his hair, flexing my fingers against his scalp.

After a few minutes, he pulled my hand away and pressed a kiss to my palm, then tucked it near his chest. "You should go to sleep. You're exhausted."

"I'm not tired anymore."

His eyes flashed up to mine. Desire swirled in their depths. In response, the desire within me began to unfurl.

"You have a concussion."

"If you keep me awake, you won't have to wake me up in an hour."

"If I kept you awake right now, I would be the biggest douche bag known to man."

"Are you turning me down?" I asked, a little bit of hurt squishing the desire.

He laughed. "Hell no."

"Then…?"

"Why is it that women get offended when men try to do the right thing?"

"What?" His convoluted answer was making my headache return.

He hooked a hand around my hip and slid me across the mattress, closing the distance between us. Then he turned onto his back and guided my head so it was pillowed on his shoulder. His arm wrapped around me, holding me snuggly at his side.

With his free arm, he clicked off the bedside lamp. Darkness plunged around us.

"Baby, get the sleep now while I'm offering it to you because the minute you become mine, sleep won't come as often."

I slid my leg between his while he gently caressed the exposed skin of my waist and then I easily drifted off to sleep.

11

Every hour he woke me.

With kisses.

I never even tried to hit him.

When he would pull away, I would clutch him back for more.

Each hour upon hour, the kisses lasted just a little bit longer.

Every hour upon hour, seduction grew thicker, wrapping around the room like a heavy fog just after a twilight rain.

It was a delicious game of foreplay, kisses stretched into touches, and touches stretched into caresses. His hands began to linger on the inside of my thighs and the hollow between my breasts. Every time he touched me, my entire body quivered. It got harder and harder to fall asleep because I wanted the sweet torment to go on and on.

I don't know what time it was when need began to overpower everything else. The curtains were drawn and the room was still dark. My hands grew bold as he lay back and tried to sleep.

I was tired of sleeping.

I started with his chest, grazing my fingers across his collarbone and down his defined chest. The pads of my fingers explored his nipples, which puckered tightly whenever I touched them too long. And then my hand dipped lower, trailing in a straight line past his belly button, and snagged on the waistband of his shorts.

There was a string there for adjusting the waist. I played with that string, occasionally brushing my knuckles across his belly. Every time I did, his muscles contracted.

Keeping my body still, lying against his side, I gently released the string and began to slip just a little bit lower.

The ridge in the center of his shorts told me he definitely wasn't asleep. Using two fingers, I brushed down the length of him.

He moaned.

Then I came back up, once again exploring the shape and hardness of him. A little bolder, I cupped ay hand around him, sliding back down toward the base.

He caught my hand.

"What are you doing, Harlow?"

"Waking you up."

"Oh, I'm awake."

"Good. I wouldn't want you to miss this."

He sucked in a breath and I smiled in the darkness.

I pushed up off the mattress and leaned over, kissing him softly and then pulling away and kissing down his neck and chest. Because I wondered what he would do, I flicked my tongue across his nipple and he groaned again.

So I did it again. And again.

And then I started to kiss lower, heading toward the waistband of his shorts.

He moved fast, catching me under the arms and dragging me back up his body. "Not so fast," he whispered. "You're not the only one who gets to play."

A little wave of thrill shot through me, and my toes curled against the mattress. He rolled me over gently, making sure there was a pillow beneath my head. And then he reached for the straps of my tank top, peeling them away, slowly lowering the shirt until my entire chest was bare.

Cam stretched the shirt down over my hips, past my legs, and then tossed it away. His skin was warm when his body came over mine and we were skin to skin, chest to chest. My nipples hardened instantly and the friction of him against me made me gasp.

His mouth claimed mine in a kiss that was more aggressive than the gentle ones that pulled me from sleep. Whatever desire was left dormant inside me came roaring out of its cage. Our tongues stroked each other with a secret kind of song that only they knew. My limbs hummed with pleasure and his chest vibrated like he was a giant cat.

His kiss traveled lower, latching onto one of my breasts and suckling the oversensitive skin until the inside of my legs tingled and began to lift off the mattress. I gripped his head as he kissed lower across my abdomen, and when he pulled at the waistband of my boxers with his teeth, my knees began to shake.

He pulled the shorts away and paused. I could feel his gaze on me. "You're not wearing any panties," he rasped.

"I never wear any to bed."

"I'm going to touch you now," he whispered. "You're going to like it."

He began in the juncture where my legs met my body, drawing a finger up each side along my vagina and making my tongue slide over my teeth. A small whimper escaped my mouth and he chuckled low.

Gently, Cam slid closer, each hand parting the folds and dipping into my most sacred place on my body. He groaned. "You're soaked."

His finger slid back and forth, up and down, and every once in while it would brush against the little bud nestled between the folds and my body would spasm involuntarily. "Not yet you don't," he said and pulled his fingers away.

When I thought I couldn't take any more, he lowered, pressing my thighs wide.

I whispered his name, unsure about what he was doing.

"It's okay, baby. I got you."

Yes. Yes, he did have me.

In fact, I was pretty sure somewhere along the line, he collected another piece of my heart.

His fingers were replaced by his mouth, and his tongue was very skilled at pleasure. His tongue was slightly rough and it built this kind of pressure inside me that just begged for release. He sucked, nipped at parts, and smoothed his lips over it all.

Cam latched onto my clitoris, at the same time slipping two fingers inside me and crooking them forward.

"Cam," I moaned, but it sounded more like a prayer.

The release came quickly, absolutely, all encompassing. My body arched off the bed like I was a graceful ballerina and I opened my mouth, but no sound came out.

The inner muscles of my vagina flexed around his fingers, and he milked it, claiming every single last drop of pleasure as his own.

I collapsed onto the bed, utterly boneless, as he covered my body with his, the rock-hard manhood held hostage beneath the fabric of his shorts strained forward and rocked against my core.

A moment ago, I thought he took all my pleasure.

I was wrong.

New desire swept me along, right into his arms, and I wrapped my legs around his hips, urging him closer, inviting him in.

He chuckled in my ear. "You are fucking amazing."

"Please don't make me wait," I whispered, grabbing him by the face and kissing him with a desperation that only a starved woman could possess.

"What do you want?" he whispered.

"You. Inside me."

He sucked in a breath. *Did that just come out of my mouth?*

Yes. Yes, it did. I wasn't about to take it back.

I ran my hands down his back, my fingers diving beneath his shorts and pushing them down. He sat up on his knees and pushed them farther, his hardness springing forth, the proof of his desire.

I wrapped my hand around it, wanting to feel it, wanting to explore it. It was the softest thing I think I'd ever touched, yet it was the hardest. My other hand came up and cupped his balls, weighing them in my palm.

Tentatively, I leaned forward, licking my tongue up the side like it was a lollipop.

"Whoa," he said, pulling back. "You can do that later."

Gently, he pressed me back into the mattress, giving me a quick kiss, and then he stood, yanking off the shorts the rest of the way and then moving around to the foot of the bed.

"What are you doing?" I asked, wanting him there with me.

I heard the sound of a zipper and then the crinkle of something.

"Just getting something to protect you with," he said, his voice completely raspy.

Several seconds later, he was back, settling between my legs and staring down at me through the darkness. "Are you sure?"

"Yes."

"I'll stop right now."

"Please, don't stop."

He came over me, wrapping me in his embrace. I could feel the head of his erection at my entrance and I tried not to be nervous. When I thought he would slide in, he didn't. Instead, he smoothed the hair away from my face and kissed me slowly, thoroughly, passionately.

"You are so beautiful," he whispered, kissing along my hairline. "So fucking beautiful."

His lips came back to mine and he joined our bodies with one long stroke. My body tensed at the slight sting of pain, and he held himself still, even though I felt the tremor in his arms, the effort in his entire body.

He kissed me again, sweeping his tongue inside my mouth and letting it linger. After several moments, my body completely relaxed and I felt a new surge of wetness between my legs. Only then did he begin to move, languid strokes at first, staying deep and stretching me out.

Then he pulled back, almost leaving me completely. I was about to protest when he surged back, filling me up totally as sensation rocked my body.

I couldn't do much but grip his biceps and moan. It was the single most stunning feeling I'd ever experienced. And he did it over and over again. Until I was panting and my hips started moving, demanding something of their own.

Up and up we went—his body carrying me higher until we were both poised at the very edge of a cliff, staring down at the endless drop.

"Together," he whispered and then with a final thrust, we both fell, plunging into never-ending bliss.

I could feel him pumping inside me; every single movement he made extended my pleasure even longer.

He collapsed beside me with a soft curse, reached for me, dragging me over his chest, and held me tightly.

"Sweet Jesus," he said. "That was…" He paused. "I don't even know what that was."

"Does that mean it was okay?" I asked, hoping it was at least half as good for him as it was for me.

He lifted me off his chest. His eyes stared at me through the early morning light. "Please tell me you loved that. Please tell me you want to do it again."

I giggled. "I loved it. I really hope we do it again. Lots of agains."

He groaned and clutched me against him. "Don't bother thinking you'll find better," he said, palming my butt. "Because you won't. That was incredible."

When I closed my eyes in pure satisfaction, I felt him reaching for something. I heard the nightstand rattle. Then the face of his cell phone lit up. "It's eight thirty. What time do you have to be at work?"

"Ten." I groaned. How was I going to get out of this bed? "I didn't think it was possible, but I think I just became even less of a morning person."

He chuckled.

"You missed surfing."

"That was better than surfing. *You* are better than surfing."

And that was how he claimed yet another piece of my heart.

*　　*　　*

We showered together. I didn't want to get my hair wet, so I pulled it into a ponytail and he was kind enough to wash my body. Some parts got *really* clean.

So I did what every thoughtful girl would do. I repaid the favor.

By the time we were done, the water was cold and I was almost late (you try being on time with a naked, hot surfer in your shower). So I rushed around the bathroom, brushing my teeth and applying lotion (with sunscreen) on my face.

After I got dressed in my Snow Cone Shack tank top and a pair of jean shorts, I took a minute to braid the front section of my hair, starting above my eye and braiding across the front all the way behind the ear. I secured the braid with a small band and pinned the rest up in a little twist on the back of my head with a gorgeous barrette that I bought one night after work at one of the nearby shops. It was handcrafted with colorful pieces of sea glass. Hopefully it would keep me cool.

"What's with all the girl food?" Cam complained as I came out of the bedroom and grabbed my bag off the counter.

"Uh, two girls live here?" I said.

"Yogurt and granola," he said, making a face and shutting the refrigerator door. "You need some man food."

"Why would we need to get some man food?" I asked casually, stepping into the kitchen.

"Because this man intends on sleeping over. A lot." He wrapped his arms around me and towed me into his chest.

I buried my faced in his shirt and grinned. "I'll share my yogurt."

He grunted. "I'm bringing over the bacon. And the Pop-Tarts."

"You eat Pop-Tarts and bacon for breakfast?"

"Man food," he growled.

"Junk food." I argued and pulled back to grab an orange and a cereal bar to throw into my bag. Then I grabbed a bottle of water. "I'm ready."

Roxie stumbled through her bedroom door as I slipped on my sandals. She looked exactly like me in the morning. One eye open, hair in a twisted mess, and walking like a zombie.

"I'm so sorry. Did we wake you up?"

"No," she mumbled, heading for the kitchen.

"Coffee's already made," I said, amused.

"I had to get up because I have to take my car to get the air-conditioner fixed. It stopped working and I am not driving that thing around in this heat with no AC."

"Yuck," I agreed. "I work until four, but I'm not on the schedule tonight at the club. So if I don't see you before you go in to work, I'll see you tomorrow."

She waved as she stuck her nose into her mug.

"You're not working tonight?" Cam said as we walked down to the parking lot.

"No, but I work tomorrow night. How about you?"

"I work tonight, off tomorrow."

"Oh, well, I'll just take my car so you don't have to rush between picking me up and then getting to work." I looked over at my car, noticing something fluttering slightly in the breeze.

I went over to it, squinting, trying to make out what it was as I approached. When I knew what it was, I stopped and stared at it, an odd feeling snaking through me.

"What's that?" Cam asked, coming up behind me.

There, pinned underneath my windshield wiper, was a one-dollar bill. "It's a dollar."

"A dollar?" Cam repeated, looking over my shoulder.

I nodded and pulled it free, looking it over to see if there was anything written on either side. There wasn't.

"That's odd," I murmured.

"Probably someone's idea of a joke."

"Yeah," I agreed, wondering what was funny about a dollar bill.

"C'mon, I'll drive you. We gotta go or you're going to be late." He took my hand and led me away from my Toyota and deposited me inside the Mustang.

I was still gripping the dollar bill as we drove to Broadway at the Beach.

I stared at it the entire way.

12

Broadway at the Beach was packed. I wasn't surprised, though, because it was the weekend and it was summer. The weather was gorgeous, clear blue sky, white puffy clouds, and the faint scent of the ocean in the air.

But like every other day in the South, it was hot. It wasn't the heat that was the killer, though. No, what was worse was the humidity. It was one of those days where the thick, stagnant air threatened to choke you. It pushed against your body, threatening to take every last drop of moisture you had in your skin and wring it out only to move on to someone new.

I was busy enough that I didn't have much time to dwell on the fact that the weather was trying to kill me. And thankfully, all the scooping of shaved ice help keep my temperature down to a level I could tolerate.

As I worked, little tendrils of hair would slip from the twist and fall down, sticking to my neck and tickling my cheek. It became very annoying and finally, I just reached up and pulled the barrette out of my hair and laid it right beside the cash register.

When the last customer walked away, my cell phone chimed and I picked it up, glancing at the screen.

"Hey, Roxie, what's up?"

"My car sucks!" she exclaimed.

I suppressed a grin. "I take it the AC is still broken?"

"It's still at the shop. Apparently I need some new part. Don't ask me what it is because my brain went buh-bye when they told me how much it cost."

"Oh, crap. How much?"

"Four hundred dollars!"

I sucked in a breath. "Damn."

"Yeah. I'm going to have to act like a ho at work tonight to pay for this."

I winced. "I'm sorry."

She let out a sigh. "It's fine. My car has to stay there overnight. I guess the part will be here in the morning. I know you're off tonight, but would you mind giving me a ride to work? I can get one of the other girls to drop me off on her way home."

"Sure, I don't have plans anyway."

"Not going out with Cam?" she said, making kissing noises on her end of the line.

My phone beeped and I pulled it away, looking down at the screen. My mother was calling. "Cam has to work tonight," I said into the phone, laughing.

"Well, maybe you should have a drink at the bar after you drop me off."

"Maybe I will."

"You two looked awful chummy this morning," she said slyly. "I saw his car outside when I came home last night and he wasn't on the couch."

"He was in my room."

Roxie made a squealing sound. "I need details."

I laughed. "Later. I'm at work."

"Fine. Later." She sighed dramatically.

We said our good-byes and I hung up. A message came up on the screen that said, "New Voicemail." A couple approached and I set the phone on the edge of the cart and opened the cooler, reaching and making two snow cones, one blue raspberry and one watermelon, then rang up their total on the register.

As they moved away, the boat that gave thrill rides tore through the water and made a sharp turn, splashing all the people in the boat who all yelled and screeched. I turned to watch their crazy antics as it spun in circles over the water.

I felt rather than saw some quick movement behind me and I turned swiftly just in time to see someone rush away from the cart.

My eyes immediately went to the register, but it was closed and didn't seem harmed. All the flavorings were still there as well. I shrugged, thinking someone probably just saw someone they were meeting and ran to catch up.

Then I noticed.

My barrette was gone.

It had been lying right there beside the register. And now the space was empty.

"Hey!" I hollered, even though I was far too late. The person was already out of sight. I rushed around the side of the cart, thinking maybe they just knocked it onto the ground.

In my haste to look, my hip caught the corner of the cart and a sharp pain cut into my side. But I barely felt it because when I hit the cart, my cell phone slid down into the still open cooler.

"Crap!" I yelled, practically diving into the ice after my phone. The cooler was almost empty—as it was almost time for my lunch break and for me to refill the cart—so I had to reach way down to the bottom where my phone lay.

It landed in a pile of slush.

I spent so much time opening and closing it this morning and it was so hot that some of the ice started to melt and drip to the bottom.

I pulled it up, holding it out and watching the water literally drip from the bottom.

"I leave you alone for a few hours…" a voice drawled behind me. It startled me and I shrieked, dropping the phone—*again*—back into the ice.

"Seriously?" I sighed.

A tan muscled arm reached around me into the cooler and pulled out my phone. "You have a towel?"

I grabbed a white towel and handed it to Cam. "It's ruined," I announced.

"I'll take it back to my place and put it in some rice."

"I don't think my phone would taste good in stir fry."

"Ha," he said, drying it off and taking out the battery. "The rice should draw out all the excess moisture."

"Do you think it will work?" I worried. I really didn't have it in the budget to buy a new phone.

"Maybe." He shrugged. "How did it get in there anyway?"

That reminded me of my barrette. I went around the front of the cart and searched the ground and beneath it for my clip. It wasn't there.

"Son of a…" I swore, letting my words trail away.

"What?"

"Someone stole my hair clip." I turned to face him. "They literally just ran off with it."

He wrinkled his nose. "Why would they do that?"

"I have no idea," I said wearily.

"Was it valuable?"

I shook my head. "It was made of sea glass. It wasn't expensive, but it was my favorite."

He wrapped an arm around my shoulders and pulled me into his side and kissed the top of my braid. "We'll get you a new one."

"What are you doing here?" I asked, pulling back.

"Taking you to lunch."

"Somewhere with air-conditioning, please."

"Johnny Rocket's?" he suggested.

I nodded. "That's perfect because it's right beside the little office where I have to refill the cart."

I packed up the cart and pushed it into the office while Cam held the door. Then I locked it up inside and we went to the little burger joint and grabbed a table in the blissful AC.

As soon as we had our food, Cam shoved about four fries in his mouth and said, "Go out on a date with me."

"I'd love to."

"Tonight."

"I thought you had to work?"

"I did. I switched with one of the other bartenders. Now I'm off tonight and I work tomorrow with you."

"You switched your schedule?"

He nodded and took a sip of his soda. "It's obvious that you miss me terribly when I'm not around. And you abuse your poor cell phone."

I laughed. "I do not abuse my cell phone."

"But you miss me horribly."

"I admit, you're not bad to have around."

"Flattery will get you everywhere," he said.

"So where are we going on our date?"

"What do you like to do?"

I shrugged and caught myself before I blurted out something like "anything so long as I'm with you." If I wasn't careful, I would be batting my eyes at him and offering to feed him grapes.

"My favorite place to hang out here is the aquarium."

"The one on the other side of Broadway?"

I nodded. "You've been there, right?"

"Not since I was a kid."

"I think it's peaceful. All the water and the fish. The colors…" He was watching me so I picked up my soda and took a drink.

"Where's the last place you went on a date?" he asked.

I swirled a fry around in my ketchup. "I haven't dated much since high school."

"You can't tell me that a girl like you doesn't get offers."

"I wasted a lot of time and energy on a guy all through high school. He was a jerk. After that, I decided to spend more time on me and not guys."

"I'm a guy," he pointed out.

"I noticed," I said as memories of this morning practically took me hostage.

"So you're spending time with me."

Yeah, I was. He was like a giant Harlow magnet that freaking pulled me in with a single touch. "Just don't turn out to be a jerk, okay?" I said playfully.

But really, I meant it. It scared me how much and how fast I grew to like him. I mean I literally gave him my virginity within days of meeting him. It was very possible I was growing attached to him. I was very vulnerable to him in ways I'd never been to anyone before. Yes, it was thrilling, but it also made me wary.

Cam had the ability to hurt me. A lot.

He abandoned his half-eaten burger and fries to slide out of the booth and stand up. I thought he was going to leave. That I somehow crossed the line with my joke that really wasn't a joke at all.

I told myself it was better this way. That finding out he was a jerk now was better than later after he stole my heart.

The fry I was eating suddenly felt like a rock, scraping down my throat.

But he didn't leave; he didn't scowl at me for offending him. He slid into my side of the booth, his hip and leg pressed right up alongside mine. Then he draped an arm across the back of the bench and used his free hand to tip up my chin so he could look into my eyes.

"You didn't give it to the wrong guy," he murmured.

"What?" I said, falling a little further into the chocolate pools that were his eyes.

"Your virginity. You didn't give it to the wrong guy. I know we moved fast. I know you probably think I'm going to disappear like the sun on a cloudy day. But I'm not going anywhere. I'd still be here if you hadn't given yourself to me. But you did. And you know that part is just one of the many pieces of you that I plan on claiming. Pieces that I never plan to let go of."

I would never have to eat again. Those words would keep me full until the day I died.

I didn't know if he was feeding me a line, but in that moment, I didn't care. I guess in life, the possibilities of getting hurt were endless. But I wanted to be the kind of person who looked fear in the face, who listened to her gut, and right now my gut was telling me that he was sincere.

I rested my head on the back of his arm and smiled. "Are you gonna kiss me or what?"

His lips crushed against mine. Like we weren't sitting in a public place with people all around. He kissed me with a heavy passion that stole my breath and stilled my heart. It was the kind of kiss that would keep him in the front of my mind for the rest of the day, even when he was out of sight.

His lips demanded nothing but gave everything, and he leaned over so he was practically wrapped around me. He tasted faintly like Cherry Coke, my favorite, and I licked into his mouth for another taste.

He pulled back, tucking a lock of hair behind my ear. "I think we better knock it off before we get kicked out."

"I have to go back to work," I said, feeling very unenthused.

"I'll help you with the cart," he said, gathering both of our trays and depositing them in the trash.

I noticed how some people eyed us as we made our way to the door. Strangely, I didn't care. I certainly wasn't embarrassed to be seen with him. I don't think any woman would be.

Outside, the heat smacked me in the face like a wet blanket. It was suffocating and heavy. My hair began to stick to my neck immediately, and I thought longingly of my sea glass barrette.

I couldn't help but wonder why someone would steal it.

*   *   *

He was standing on the other end of the wooden bridge when my replacement showed up at the cart and I was able to leave.

Both his forearms were leaning on the railings, and he looked over the side of the bridge down into the water, where he was dropping little round pellets of fish food. He wasn't watching me, but I knew he was aware of my presence because of the way his body was slightly angled, not quite entirely toward the water. Instead, the side of his hip turned out slightly and the arm closest to me didn't lean as far or as heavily on the railing as his other.

When I got within a few feet of him, he looked over. His coffee-colored gaze speared me and my belly did a summersault. Then it did another. The corner of his mouth kicked up and he reached out, pulling me in so my back was against his front and we were both staring down at the dark water.

Only when I was settled oh so close did he lean his free arm back against the railing, effectively caging me between him and the bridge.

"Hey," he murmured, his breath tickling the side of my ear.

"Hey, yourself."

He pulled his left fist in and opened it up in front of me, revealing a palm full of the fish food. "Wanna help?"

The pads of my fingers brushed against his, and I pinched some of the pebbles and sprinkled them down into the water. Very large, very bright orange and red fish bobbed at the surface, opening up carnivorous mouths to greedily swallow the food.

We stood there silently, our bodies touching, saying nothing until his palm was empty.

Sex with Cam this morning had been amazing, a truly incredible experience, but I was realizing that this moment right here, where we were calm and still together, was the kind of moment that drew us even closer in ways that sex never could.

Chemistry between two people was one thing… but this… this feeling that was bubbling up inside me and making everything feel trembly and excited was something completely different.

It was more than chemistry.

He leaned down and pressed a kiss to my shoulder, his lips searing my skin and making my eyes slide shut.

"Date starts now," he told me.

"Now?"

"Yeah, now."

"But I'm all sweaty and gross from work."

"There is nothing gross about you."

"Sweat is gross."

"Sweat is hot, especially when I'm the one that makes your skin slick with it."

I shivered in his hold and he chuckled, knowing exactly where my mind just traveled.

"C'mon, I'll drive you home so you can shower."

He linked one of our hands together and then pulled away, tugging me alongside him as we weaved through the crowds underneath the hot summer sky. A little thrill went through me when we walked up to his bike.

He reached for his helmet and I shook my head vehemently. "Oh no. That thing weighs like fifty pounds."

"It protects you."

"But when I wear it, I can't lean all the way against you."

He pursed his lips and studied me. The he sighed dejectedly. "Fine. But I'm going to drive like a granny."

I grinned and climbed on behind him after he strapped the helmet to the back.

"Aren't you going to wear it?"

"I would look like the biggest douche alive if I drove around with a helmet on my head and not on my girl's."

My girl's.

I swear everything that came out of his mouth turned me into a giant pile of mush.

"Hold on," he said and started the bike as my arms wound around his waist. As we pulled out of the parking lot, I leaned up against him, pressing my cheek to his back and watching the scenery slowly pass.

I was really starting to like this bike.

I was a little disappointed when he pulled into the parking lot of my building and parked. I sat there even after the bike shut off, with my arms wrapped around him. Then I sighed. I was acting like a stalker. I pulled back, but he reached down and grasped my arms, still holding them around him. "Just another minute," he said.

I held on to him until he released my arms and swung off the bike.

"I'm going to run home and shower and change. I'll be back in an hour to pick you up."

"Okay," I said, walking up the steps to my apartment and turning around at the door to wave back at him. He was watching me and only after I went inside did I hear the bike start up and drive away.

Roxie was sitting on the couch, reading a gossip magazine. "Hey," I called on my way into the kitchen for a cold bottle of water.

"Did you know that Kim Kardashian got bangs?" she asked.

"No, but my life is complete now that I do."

She laughed as I joined her in the living room, dropping down on the other end of the sofa and propping up my feet.

"Where's Cam?"

"He's coming back. We have a date."

"I thought he had to work."

"He traded shifts and now he's off too."

She grinned. "He's got it bad."

I laughed. "I hope so," I confided.

"He's a good guy. I'm happy for you."

"Hey, have you had any trouble with Craig?"

"He's tried to call a couple times, but I've been ignoring the calls and deleting the messages."

That reminded me of my waterlogged phone and the message I didn't get to listen to. "Stay strong. He'll give up eventually when he realizes you aren't going to put up with him anymore."

"Hopefully sooner rather than later," she said, looking back down at her magazine. "Ooh, look, Ian Somerhalder got a new puppy!"

I laughed. "I have to take a shower. He's going to be here soon." I dug around in my bag and pulled out my car keys. "Here, you can just take my car to work. I'm not going to need it anyway. That way you won't have to ask anyone for a ride home."

"Really?" Roxie said, reaching out to take the keys.

"Absolutely."

"I'm so glad we met."

"Me too." I agreed, meaning it. I had a feeling that Roxie and I were going to be really good friends.

13

True to his word, an hour later he rang the bell at the door. I ran to open it, butterflies fluttering around inside me as I went.

He held a glass jar with a bow around it. "Brought you something," he said, grinning.

"A jar of rice?" I said, spying the long white grains inside.

"Not just any jar of rice, but *the* rice that will save your phone."

"Super hero rice?" I said, taking the jar. "Now that's a gift."

"I thought it was better than flowers," he said, shutting the door and following me into the kitchen where I set my present. "Well, that and flowers would have just been a bunch of stems after the trip on my bike."

"You brought your bike?" I said, excited.

"Of course. Any excuse to get those arms around me…" He reached for me, giving me a long, slow kiss.

"Thanks for my present," I said when he pulled away. My voice was breathless and my heart raced.

"Hopefully tomorrow your phone'll be working."

"I hope so too." I started to turn away to grab my stuff. "Let me get my bag and we can go."

"You don't need it."

"But it has my money and my—" I protested, but he cut me off.

"You don't need any money. Tonight is on me."

No phone. No purse. No cash. Nothing but Cam and me for the night? That was a plan I could fully get behind. "Thank you," I said as he took my hand and towed me toward the apartment door.

"Eh, it's just my way of making sure you are all mine tonight."

Oh, I was his all right. More than he realized.

I marveled at the way my hand tucked in his felt as we made our way down the stairs and across the parking lot to his bike. The way his fingers curled around mine protectively, possessively, it felt like it belonged there, like it fit. It was like he wanted everyone to know I was his and he wasn't going to give me up. I never thought such a simple thing could make me feel so much.

He was the first to climb on the bike, gripping the handlebars and holding it steady for me to get on behind him.

"I guess I shouldn't have worn a skirt," I mused when I attempted to sit on the warm leather. It wasn't going so well for me. I was dressed in a long jersey knit skirt that was tie-dyed with navy blue and white. I wore a loose-fitting white tank top layered over a snug navy-colored tank and tucked the front of the white tank into the waistband of the skirt. To finish it off, I added a long silver chain with a couple colorful feathers on the end as a pendant. I styled my chestnut-colored hair straight and long.

"Maybe I should change," I said with a laugh when I couldn't spread my legs over the bike because of the skirt.

Cam chuckled and swiftly stood, reached down, and bunched the skirt up around my thighs, tucking the extra fabric beneath my bottom, and settled back between my legs like he belonged there.

I wasn't about to complain.

He took me to dinner at a place on the water. We sat outside on a deck and watched the sea as ocean breezes swirled around us, and we ate seafood Alfredo and breadsticks. He told me about his parents, his life, and how he got his job at the Mad Hatter.

He asked me about my favorite color (green), my favorite movie (*Pretty Woman*), and then I told him about my plans to someday become a career counselor.

The conversation was easy and we actually had a lot in common. He was quick to smile, and if there was a break in the conversation, it was never uncomfortable. After dinner we went mini golfing (there were only like five thousand mini golf places here in Myrtle Beach) at a place with giant dinosaurs and a small waterfall that we spent more time kissing behind than we did actually golfing.

When we did golf, he got a hole in one and I lost my ball… which led to us having to look for it… behind the waterfall. We didn't find my ball, but I discovered that he wasn't hiding it anywhere in his shorts.

By the time dinner and golf was over, the sky was dark and I was more relaxed than I'd felt in a long time. "I had a really good time," I told him when we were walking toward his bike.

"Good. But the date's not over yet."

"It's not?"

"Nope. One more place left to go."

"Where?"

He smiled mischievously and patted the seat of the bike. We ended up at Broadway at the Beach. "Most of the shops are going to be closing here, Cam," I said, thinking surely we weren't going to go out to eat again.

"Good thing we aren't going shopping."

He led me past the giant water fountain in front of the aquarium that had giant statues of stingrays coming up out of the water. "I think they close in like fifteen minutes."

"I know," he said secretively.

He didn't stop to buy our tickets. He merely approached the ticket counter where one of the girls that was always working saw us and pointed at the door. It buzzed when we neared and he pulled it open and motioned for me to go ahead.

I gave him a quizzical look on my way past.

I was momentarily distracted by the large freestanding tank that greeted us on the way in. It was filled with colorful tropical-looking fish that moved around the tank—some in a hurry and some taking their time.

The building was very large, with tall ceilings and a fairly open concept. Straight ahead was a ramp that led down into the lower area where the tanks and feeding shows were. Along the way, they also had a few separate rooms dedicated to certain topics of interest. Over to the left was the gift shop, filled to the brim with stuffed animals, T-shirts, and various memorabilia. Beyond the gift shop was an area that led up from the lower level and just above that was the stingray and horseshoe crab tank where visitors could place their hands in the water for a chance to touch the fish. Also on the upper level was the snack café.

We watched the fish in the tank near the entrance for a moment. Then he took my hand and led me down the ramp toward the big tanks. It was very quiet in here at this time of night. The crowds were gone and the building was just about empty. There were a few employees bustling around, cleaning up, and doing whatever the employees did at closing time.

"Did they know we were coming?" I asked him, wondering if that was why they didn't charge us to get in. Or maybe it was because they were closing and we were going to have to leave anyway.

He smiled slyly. "They might've had an idea I was bringing you by."

"Hmmmm," I said, pondering his sneakiness.

"You must come here a lot. I thought this would take some convincing, but the minute I said your name, they knew exactly who I meant and they didn't hesitate to agree."

"Agree to what, exactly?" I asked, stopping and turning, giving him my full attention.

"Just a private tour of the aquarium."

My mouth fell open and he grinned. "We have this whole place to ourselves?"

He shrugged. "Pretty much. There are a couple employees left cleaning and doing stuff in the back. We won't see them though."

"You planned a private tour of the aquarium for me?" I said, awe spreading through my chest like warm waves across the sand.

"You said this was your favorite place." He unlinked our hands to drag his knuckles down my cheek.

This was easily the nicest, most romantic thing anyone had ever done for me. Ever. I didn't even know what to say. "It is my favorite place. I—thank you so much, Cam."

"I figured I better do something good and not screw up anymore."

I gave him a puzzled look. "Anymore?"

He ran his thumb along the underside of my lip. "Did you know your top lip is just slightly bigger than the bottom one?"

"No," I said, fighting the urge to suck his thumb into my mouth.

"It is. It's so fucking sexy it drives me insane. It screams for me to suck it."

That sent a rush of desire through me. God, the things he did to me. "You think you screwed something up?" I asked, pulling his hand away before I attacked him right here.

"I've done everything backward with you."

"How?"

"I met you in a strip club—the worst place to meet girls. Then I took you to the beach, almost drowned you, then slept with you—took your virginity—before I even asked you out on a date. This is our first date, Harlow, and I've already spent the night with you."

"Technically, the morning you almost drowned me was our first date."

"Dates that end up with someone in the medical center do not count as dates."

I laughed. "You know what I think?"

"What?" He tucked the hair behind my ear.

"You have done everything right. I can't imagine doing this any other way."

"I'm serious when I tell you I don't want you to think I'm only after you for your sexy body."

"I can see that," I said, pulling him along toward a big tank full of jellyfish. "But I think me and sexy in the same sentence is a stretch. Adam probably gave me tonight off because he was afraid I would ruin his busiest night of the week at the club."

"You definitely have the goods, babe. You just need a little more confidence to put it all on display."

"The only person I really want to put everything on display for is you," I said shyly.

He groaned. "Stop turning me on, woman, and look at the fish."

We walked through the darkened hallways with the portal windows and larger display windows, studying the fish, the sharks, and the squid. The fish seemed more relaxed than usual and I wondered if it was because they knew the day was winding down or because the crowds were gone.

Either way, being here at this time of night was so special and incredible. The only light came from the tanks and the small lighting lining the floor. The large room with the tank where they did the dive shows had some neon lighting and a large flat screen that played photos and facts about certain kinds of fish featured in the tanks.

We walked around, slowly, whispering and pointing at all the fish, and every so often Cam would press me up against a wall and bury his tongue in my mouth.

All night there had been little touches, steamy kisses, and long lingering looks exchanged and it served as foreplay and my body began to come alive in ways that only Cam could inspire.

"Oh, this is my favorite part of the entire place!" I said excitedly when we neared the conveyor belt on the floor that you stood on and it slid around, taking you through an underwater tunnel. It was stunning. As we moved, fish swam over our heads and alongside us, making me feel like I was literally part of the undersea world.

"Every time I come here, there's something new to see. It's ever-changing, yet it stays the same."

"Yeah, I can see why you like it so much. I forgot how cool it was in here."

I pointed out one of the biggest sharks they had here as it swam above us. We stepped off the conveyor belt and into a darkened hallway leading to another tank. Instead of walking on through, he leaned against the wall and spread his knees apart, pulling me between them. His hands were in my hair instantly, running through the silky strands, and he lifted my face to his and slanted his mouth over mine. He kissed me, turning his head one way and then the other. Each time the kiss was equally assaulting to my senses but in a whole new way.

He made good on his earlier words and sucked my upper lip into his mouth, kneading it with his tongue. An involuntary moan erupted in the back of my throat and I rose up on tiptoes, trying to get even closer.

His hands slid down my body and cupped my butt, squeezing and pulling me farther into him as he grinded the unmistakable hardness in his jeans against me.

Moisture slicked my panties, my body almost demanding him. My muscles began to quiver and my knees started to turn to Jell-O as the kiss went on and on and on.

I slid my fingers beneath the hem of his white cotton polo and lifted it, ducking my head and licking up the center of his abs and pressing soft kisses all along his abdomen. He groaned and relaxed against the wall, his hands falling to his sides, my mouth moved upward and latched onto one of his nipples as I rolled my tongue around it, teasing it into a rock hard point.

"Harlow," he murmured, gently pulling me back. "Baby, you have to stop. I'm going to go crazy."

I made a sound and tried to get close to him again. "It isn't my fault you make me crazy," I told him.

He chuckled and took my hand, pulling his shirt back down. "C'mon."

I thought he was going to lead me toward the exit. He didn't.

Instead, he led me back through the passageways and across the center main floor where various attractions were waiting for us to explore. We didn't stop; he just kept going, his feet quickening with every step he took.

"Where are we going?" I asked just as we rounded the corner to the largest tank in the place. It was the tank where they did the dive shows. It was completely floor to ceiling and in a room by itself with two hallways leading away from either side.

He pulled me around the corner, toward the right, and pushed me up against the wall (the giant tank was off to our right). His mouth was on mine and his kiss hinted at a crazed desperation that hadn't been there earlier.

"How do you expect me to get through an entire date when your hot little mouth wraps around my nipple and sucks with determined pressure?" he said between kisses.

I pushed my hands through his blond locks, enjoying their thickness against my fingers. I didn't say anything because he was kissing me again and it was so good. He tore his mouth away and then used his hands to yank down my tops, exposing my breasts as a feast for his eyes.

Using his hands, he cupped them, pushing them up and together, and began lavishing kisses on them. My vision turned blurry because the pleasure was so intense. My head fell back against the wall and I moaned, arching against him.

He brought his hips forward without lifting his mouth so his arousal grinded against me, urging me on, taunting me with its need.

"Cam," I begged, needing more than he was giving.

He lifted his head, pressing the softest kiss to my lips, and then our eyes locked.

He bent down, picking up the hem of my skirt and sliding it up my legs, past my knees, to bunch it around my hips. His fingers delved into the edges of my panties as he caressed the moist sensitive skin of my secret place.

I whimpered.

"I love your responses," he whispered. "I want you now, baby. Can I have you right now?"

I nodded, unable to form even a single syllable to reply.

He lifted me, sliding my back against the wall, and my legs wrapped around his waist as my ankles crossed, keeping me in place. He kissed me again, ravaging my mouth with hot, moist kisses that had me rocking against his stomach, already searching for release.

One arm held me as the other hand delved beneath my skirt, past my panties, and a single finger slid right inside me.

I bit my bottom lip to keep from crying out, and when his finger began to move, it wasn't enough so I leaned forward and sank my teeth into his shoulder right through his shirt.

Just when I thought I might explode, he pulled his hand away and undid his shorts. He reached into his back pocket and pulled out a packet and used his teeth to rip it open.

"Do you think anyone will see us?" I murmured, desire making my voice thick.

"Just the fish, sweetheart."

"I like that name," I said as he pulled a condom free.

"Yeah?" he whispered, reaching between us. "Help me out with this, sweetheart."

I pulled my hands from around his neck and used them to roll the condom onto his rigid length.

When I was done, he wrapped both arms around me again and used his body as leverage to keep me against the wall.

"This isn't going to be like last time. This is going to be faster, harder. If I hurt you, even just a little, you tell me, okay? I'll stop."

I nodded as he pulled my underwear to the side and slid all the way in. I couldn't help the groan that ripped from my throat as I felt him fill me completely. The sensations were so different from before because the angles were completely new. He went inside me so far that I swore I could feel him at the bottom of my belly.

His arm muscles were shaking as he looked down. "Are you okay?"

"More," I told him. "I want more."

He chuckled and grabbed me around the ribs, sliding my body up and down along the length of him. Everything within my body turned to liquid. I would have slid right down onto the floor if he wasn't holding me up.

The sensation of his hardness moving along my softness as my muscles clenched around him was almost my undoing. He began to move faster, to sink himself even deeper until one of his palms slapped against the wall beside my head and I grinded my hips down on him as he began to pulse.

Shock waves of pleasure washed over me as I continued to grind against him, tiny noises escaping as the orgasm rolled through.

Cam buried his head in my neck, his body straining against me and his breath hot on my skin. The hand that had been against the wall came down, and he caressed the outside of my leg as we both calmed our racing hearts.

My vision began to clear and I stared at the still swimming fish like an earthquake hadn't just rocked this room, as if they hadn't even noticed the way passion literally erupted out of the both of us.

"Did I hurt you?" he asked, lifting me just a little and slipping out of my body.

"No. I loved it." My feet hit the floor and my skirt fell down around me. My top was still half pulled down and he adjusted it so nothing showed.

"Think there's some kind of club for people who do it in the aquarium?"

I giggled.

He adjusted himself, zipping up his shorts and then taking my hand. We walked quietly through the building until we came to a bathroom. "I'll be right back," he said, disappearing in the men's room.

I went into the ladies' room and cleaned up a little and washed my hands. I barely recognized the flush-faced girl in the mirror with wide, dancing eyes. I'd never looked this happy. I'd never felt this alive.

Cam was still in the men's room when I came out so I walked up the little path where the stingrays were swimming and slipped two fingers into the cool water and held them there, waiting to see if one would come up and allow me to pet it.

I listened to the water gently lapping against the sides of the tank and watched as one of the rays began lazily making its way closer. Cam came up behind me, wrapping his arms around me, and then easily sinking two fingers into the water alongside mine. The stingray glided over, right up against us, dragging its smooth body along our outstretched hands.

When it was gone, he kissed the top of my head and handed me a towel to wipe the water off my hands.

"Let's go in here before we leave," he said, guiding me toward the gift shop.

"Hey," he said softly from a few feet away. "Look at this,"

I went to his side and peered around him at a wrapped gift on the glass display counter. "What's that?"

"It has your name on it," he said, lifting a small white tag that definitely had my name on it.

It was a small square box wrapped simply in brown paper and tied with a white bow. I picked it up and smiled as I untied the ribbon and lifted the lid to the box.

I stared down at what was nestled inside. "It's beautiful," I whispered, like I might disturb the beauty of the gift.

"You like it?" he asked.

I reached in and pulled out the jewelry. The bracelet itself was crafted out of leather cording, the color of a crystal-clear jade-green sea. The cording was braided all around until it stopped at a small silver clasp. In the center of the bracelet was a round circle with a white background and a hard, clear resin top. Inside the circle were the words *Pura Vida* in the same green color as the leather.

"Did you make this?" I asked, fingering the center and then exploring the braided leather.

"Yeah. It's not much,"

"Are you kidding? This is everything."

"So you like it?" he asked nervously.

I handed it to him and then held out my wrist so he could clasp it around. "I can't think of anything I would like more. The fact that you made it only makes it even better."

He clasped it and then I pulled my hand away, turning it over so I could stare down at the way it wrapped around my wrist.

I threw my arms around his neck, reaching up on tiptoes and hugging him as hard as I dared. "You're really good with your hands," I murmured, pressing a kiss to the underside of his jaw.

He chuckled. "Yeah, my hands know how to please."

"I still can't believe you planned all this."

"You're worth it."

"How do you know?" I asked him, tilting my head to the side.

"My gut told me. It's never steered me wrong."

I stared down at the bracelet again. I was never going to take it off.

"You ready?" he asked.

I nodded.

On our way out, he picked up a small stuffed stingray—a white one with brown spots—and handed it to me. Then he jogged back to the counter, laid some cash on the table, and then we left the aquarium to walk out into the night.

The Broadway was almost entirely empty and the fountain was lit up with pink and blue lights. The sound of the water as it poured from the top sounded like a rainstorm on a sunny day.

I held the stingray between us on the ride back to my place, keeping my cheek pressed against his back.

The night air actually felt cool as it raced over my skin and pulled at my hair. But I didn't care. I would sit here and freeze to death before I even thought about moving.

The parking lot at my building was full, most people home for the night already, so he had to park a little farther away than usual.

"How late is it?" I wondered when I noticed my Toyota parked nearby. "Roxie's already home."

"I haven't looked at the clock at all," he said. "It can't be two a.m. though."

"Maybe she got off early."

"Probably."

We stopped on the sidewalk at the bottom of the stairs. "Do you want to come in?" I asked him, looking up through my lashes.

"I don't want to move too fast and mess this up," he said, his eyes sweeping over my face.

"I think we should just stop worrying about moving too fast and just go at our own pace," I said, meaning it. What were the rules for this anyway? Were there any? I mean, I spent almost four years with a guy that I felt like I was waiting for the perfect time for everything. But that time never came. Because he wasn't the right guy.

I wasn't sure if Cam was the right guy, but after tonight, I was thinking he might be.

He opened his mouth to reply, but I never heard what he said.

Because a shrill scream pierced the night.

It came from my apartment.

14

As Roxie screamed, the door to my apartment flew open, slamming against the wall with a sharp cracking sound. I hadn't noticed until that moment that the porch light above our door was out and so was the closest street lamp nearby.

A man in dark clothing and a ski mask rushed out of the apartment and lunged down the stairs. Roxie was still screaming, and I began to worry she was hurt.

"Roxie!" I cried, rushing forward.

Cam yanked me back, shoving me behind him, and then rushed forward after the man who was running across the parking lot and disappeared behind the building. Cam stopped pursuing and turned back, torn between leaving me and chasing the man.

I rushed up the stairs into the apartment, yelling my roommate's name, flipping on the lights as I went.

Thankfully, they all turned on. Roxie was sitting in the living room in the middle of the path between our bedrooms. She was on the floor with her back against the wall and her knees pulled into her chest.

"Oh my God, Roxie," I said, falling to my knees in front of her. "What happened? Are you okay?"

Cam rushed into the apartment behind me, his eyes locking on the both of us, then narrowing as he went from room to room searching the place for any more unwanted intruders.

"Roxie," I said again, trying to calm my frantic voice.

"I'm okay," she said, her voice a little shaky. "He didn't do anything to me."

"I saw him run out of here. What happened? What are you doing home so early?"

"I wasn't feeling well. I have a horrible headache. I only got a couple hours of sleep last night, and I sat at that godforsaken garage half the day and they didn't have any air-conditioning either."

"You're probably overheated."

She nodded. "Adam sent me home. He told me I looked like shit."

"Wasn't that charming of him?" I observed.

She laughed and it turned into a sob.

"He must have been watching the apartment, waiting for me. The porch light was out when I came home and I just figured the bulb was burnt out. When I was trying to unlock the door, I heard the crunch of glass under my feet and I realized that the bulb had been broken."

I made sympathetic noises as horror raced over my skin, leaving behind a fine coating of chills.

"I turned to leave, but he was already coming up the steps. I tried to get inside and lock him out, but he shoved the door open and tackled me. I managed to kick him and run away, but he caught me again and was dragging me through the living room when I fell."

"Oh my God," I said, horrified. I couldn't help but wonder if he planned to rape her.

A cold bottle of water appeared before Roxie and she looked up at Cam, who offered it to her. "Thank you," she murmured and took it, taking a sip and drawing in a deep breath. "I yelled at him to please stop and to leave me alone. And it was so weird. Whenever I said it, he paused, like he was actually considering my request."

"And then what happened?" Cam asked.

"He got up and ran out the front door. Then you got here."

I nodded. "We saw him run away."

"I would have caught the bastard, but I was afraid to leave you ladies alone."

"Thank God you showed up when you did," Roxie said and started to cry.

I reached over and put my arms around her. She leaned her head onto my shoulder and kept crying.

"Are you sure he didn't hurt you?" Cam said, reaching out to touch her shoulder.

She flinched and he pulled away. "I think so," she said, still crying.

"I'm calling the police," he said and got to his feet, pulling out his cell phone.

There was a noise by the still-open front door. Roxie screamed and Cam spun around defensively.

"What the hell is going on?" Adam said, stepping through, his eyes going straight to Roxie huddled against the wall. "Roxie?"

At the sound of his voice, she started sobbing even harder. His eyes grew wide and he looked at Cam for an explanation.

"Someone broke in and attacked her."

Adam's face went completely white. Then he strode across the room and reached down toward her. She let go of me and moved willingly into his arms. He picked her up off the floor as Cam spoke quietly on the phone.

I watched Adam carry her over to the couch and sit down with her in his lap. She wasn't a small girl. She was pretty tall, but she looked small sitting there in his lap.

"Hey," he murmured, trying to pull her away from his chest. She clung to him, not budging, not wanting to move. "I'm just trying to see if you're hurt," he told her quietly. "Let me see."

She let him pull her back and he looked her over. So did I. There didn't appear to be any damage that I could see.

"Did he rape you?" Adam asked, his voice hard.

"No!" she said sharply, then collapsed against his chest.

"It's a good fucking thing. I'm going to kill him," he said, his voice deadly calm. It was actually kind of intimidating.

Roxie started to cry harder and Adam swore beneath his breath. "I didn't mean to scare you. Calm down. I'm not going anywhere."

He continued to talk to her, trying to soothe her. I wandered around, letting them have some privacy (for some reason it seemed like I was intruding on a private moment), looking for missing items or anything broken. Everything looked exactly the same as when I left.

Even my jar of rice was still sitting untouched on the kitchen counter.

"Cops are on their way," Cam told the room when he hung up his phone. He walked over and shut the front door, locking it for good measure.

Roxie's sobs had quieted and Adam was still cradling her in his lap. "I shouldn't have sent you home. This wouldn't have happened," he said.

"We would have had to come home sometime," I told him.

"You girls shouldn't be living here alone," Adam snapped.

"It was him," Roxie murmured.

"Him who?" I asked, going around the couch to look at her.

"Craig. It was Craig."

Adam let forth a string of cuss words that should have earned him an award. Even Cam let a couple loose as he sat in the only other chair in the room besides the couch.

"So that was Craig that was here?" I asked, trying to make sense of it all.

She nodded. "I think so."

"You think he was trying to scare you?" I asked.

"I don't know. Maybe."

"Roxie, are you sure it was Craig? Did he say something to you?"

She made a frustrated sound and her grip on Adam's shirt tightened. "No, he didn't. I don't... I'm not sure. But who else could it have been?"

Who indeed?

Still, it was clear Roxie was scared. And it was clear it was Craig she was scared of.

Adam and I exchanged a look. "Roxie," I said, wetting my lips with my tongue and sitting on the couch beside them. "Was Craig ever…? Did he abuse you?"

She started crying again and buried her face in Adam's neck. His arms tightened around her.

I would take that as a yes.

Adam's eyes were hard as he stared over her head at the wall.

"Why aren't you at the club?" Cam asked Adam.

"Because she looked really bad when I sent her home. I was worried about her driving so I wanted to make sure she got home okay."

A few minutes later, there was a knock on the door. I got up to answer it, but Cam waved me back as he pulled it open, his body tense. When his shoulders relaxed, I knew it was the police.

"Police are here," I told Roxie.

"I don't want to get them involved," she said, wide-eyed.

"Why?"

"It'll just make him angrier."

Adam's hand clenched into a fist at Roxie's back. "You need to talk to the cops, Rox."

"Ma'am." A tall lanky officer came into the room. "We'd like to talk to you about what happened here tonight."

Roxie nodded and climbed off Adam's lap. She straightened her yoga pants and T-shirt and faced the lanky cop and the stocky one coming up behind him. "I'll tell you what I can. It all happened so fast."

We all listened to her repeat what happened and then repeat it again. The more she talked, she became even less sure it was Craig. She didn't see his face, and he didn't even yell at her (apparently he always yelled at her). I could see the fear in her eyes, but I also saw a little bit of doubt. It was the doubt that worried me most.

The police officers were still asking her questions when Cam opened the front door and looked outside. I went across the room and glanced around the open door.

"Are you leaving?"

"Get back inside," he said gently. "No, I'm not leaving."

"What are you doing?"

"You have a broom? I'll sweep up this glass from the busted bulb."

I went into the kitchen to get the dust pan and brush and gave it to him. "I can do that in the morning."

"I don't want you to get cut."

I leaned in the door frame and watched him sweep up the glass from the light of the kitchen and living room. My eyes scanned the parking lot as he worked, looking for shadows within shadows, looking for anything that might indicate if someone was out there… watching.

Once the glass was cleaned up, he tossed it away and placed the dustpan back in the kitchen. I was still standing in the door, staring outside. "Come away from there." He spoke quietly, taking my hand and pulling me away from the darkness.

He closed the door behind me and grazed his knuckles down the side of my face. "Don't be scared."

"I'm not." My eyes went to Roxie talking to the police. What if they couldn't prove it was Craig? Would they just leave him out there so he could come back?

"We'd like to take your statements," the stocky officer said as he came up behind Cam and me.

By the time we both gave our statement and Roxie finished answering questions, it was really late and I was exhausted. Roxie was pale, had dark circles under her eyes, and when she lifted her water to her lips, her hands shook.

"You should go to bed," I told her, handing her a bottle of Motrin to go with her water.

"I'm not sure I'll be able to sleep."

"I'm staying tonight," Cam told her. "You girls won't be alone."

She nodded.

"I'm staying too," Adam announced.

Roxie and I both turned to look at him. "You're going to sleep here tonight?" I asked.

He nodded. "I'll take the couch." He glanced at Roxie. "Just in case anyone needs anything."

Roxie visibly relaxed at Adam's announcement, so I figured it was a good idea. I found a couple extra blankets and Roxie gave him a pillow off her bed. Cam and I said goodnight as Adam was using his phone to check in at the club.

After I washed my face and brushed my teeth, I went into the bedroom to change. I tossed my dirty clothes in my laundry basket and pulled on a pair of striped boxers and a purple tank top. Cam was in the bathroom, and I waited for him by going to my vanity and picking up my brush, running it over my hair and smiling at the glimpse of the reflection of the bracelet Cam gave me.

Tonight had been so wonderful. Not even all the bad stuff that happened since we got home could take away all the giddiness I felt about my first official date with Cam.

After all the tangles in my hair were gone and it was shining around my shoulders, I set down the brush.

Something caught my eye.

There on the vanity near my brush, propped in front of the mirror, was my sea glass barrette.

The one that was stolen earlier today.

My stomach churned and my palms became slick with nervous sweat.

I knew then the reason nothing, besides Roxie, was disturbed tonight when someone broke into this house.

They weren't here to steal anything.

They came to leave something behind.

15

The next couple days went by in a blur. I walked around on autopilot, going to work, making snow cones, dancing (let's face it, I would never be a great stripper), and serving drinks at the Mad Hatter. In between all that, Roxie and I obsessively checked the locks on the door and stared out into the shadows of the parking lot at night.

I questioned Roxie again about the man who muscled his way into our home, and she seemed very convinced it was Craig. Both of us were waiting on pins and needles to hear what the police would tell us after they paid him a visit.

Shouldn't they have done that by now?

Shouldn't we have heard something?

Did it really matter? Because the more I thought, the more I obsessed, the more I began to think that it wasn't Craig. I was beginning to think that Roxie's visitor was meant for me.

But that seemed crazy, so crazy that I hadn't confided my fears to anyone. Why would someone come after me? I was a broke college student who spent all her time working. Sure, I had friends, but no one I really hung out with. My roommate had been the only person I spent time with outside of school, and she moved to another state last month to get a job with her shiny new bachelor's degree.

It was the reason I was so happy to have met Roxie. She seemed like good friend material. And Cam... Cam was perfect boyfriend material. Not that we were official or anything. We hadn't really had time to have the "talk." Plus, it was all still pretty new. There was no reason to rush things. Yeah, okay, some people might say we rushed things already by having sex so fast, but the way I see it is I'm twenty-one years old, a woman. I go to school, work two jobs, and take care of myself. Cam makes me feel things I never have before. My body practically purrs whenever he's near. His touch scrambles my thoughts and turns me into Jell-O. I might not love him (not yet anyway), but I was old enough to make my own decisions.

I was beyond thrilled when my shift at the snow cone cart was finished and I could go home. I spent most of the day zoning about the barrette and searching the crowds for faces that I might recognize or for a stranger who seemed intrigued by me.

I was tired. Neither Roxie nor I had been sleeping well, and I secretly missed Cam. It seemed silly because spending just two nights in his arms was enough to make me reach for him in the middle of night.

As I trudged through the heat toward the parking lot, someone grabbed me from behind and I stiffened, a shriek clawing its way out of my throat as I prepared to scream and kick.

"Harlow, it's me," Cam said, releasing me and stepping back. "I didn't mean to scare you. I called out your name."

I spun around and launched myself at him, hugging him hard around the waist. "I'm sorry, I must not have heard you."

"You okay?" he asked, looking down. "Are you still upset about the other night?" He brushed a finger beneath my eye where they were no doubt shadowed with dark circles.

I shrugged.

"Talk to me."

"I didn't know you were coming to see me today," I said, changing the subject.

"I finished up the board I was working on this afternoon and figured I'd come see my girl."

I knew it was just an expression, but every time he called me his girl, or sweetheart, something inside me melted just a little bit more. "I'm glad you came."

He leaned down and kissed me. His kiss was like a really good book or movie. It completely transported me to another place. It took me out of my own head, and I did nothing but get lost in him.

"I needed that," I murmured when he lifted his head.

"You need ice cream too."

"I do?"

He nodded and draped an arm across my shoulders, fitting me alongside his body and steering me toward Ben and Jerry's. He ordered a massive serving of Phish Food (chocolate ice cream swirled with gooey marshmallow and caramel with fudge fish) swimming inside a giant waffle bowl. I had no idea where he was going to put it all, but it was definitely going to be interesting to watch. I ordered a scoop of chocolate mint crunch in a regular-sized cone and then we sat in the corner of the scoop shop at a tiny round table.

"Seriously, how are you going to eat that?" I mused, watching him shovel a huge bite of the sweet treat into his mouth.

"It's Phish Food," he declared like that somehow explained everything. Then he scooped up a fudge fish and held the spoon to my lips.

I opened my mouth and he slid the spoon between my teeth and then pulled it back, my lips dragging across the cold plastic as he pulled. His eyes darkened as he watched my mouth move.

When the spoon was gone, I pulled up my cone and started licking across the top and around the edges.

"Are you trying to kill me?" he asked, leaning over the table, his eyes still on my mouth.

"Definitely not." I held the cone out to him and he licked up the side of it slowly. After he swallowed, he lowered his voice and leaned even closer. "You taste better."

I wagged my eyebrows at him and he chuckled.

He looked so good today with a navy-blue baseball hat turned backward covering up his blond hair, rocking the beachy tan that never went away, and wearing a white T-shirt with a pair of navy-blue board shorts with a wide gray stripe down each side.

"Have you gotten any sleep the last couple days?"

I nodded. "Some."

"Have you heard from the cops?"

"No," I said, frowning. "I really thought they would have said something to Roxie by now."

"What else is bothering you?" he asked, studying me.

"How do you know there's something else?"

"I can see it in your eyes. You've been kind of quiet since the other night. What's bothering you?"

Someone bumped into our table and I jumped back.

Cam frowned. "Come on, let's go somewhere else to talk."

We went to the beach, both of us discarding our shoes to the back seat of my car and taking our ice cream to walk onto the sand and wander along the water's edge. The heat was more bearable here because of the strong wind that came off the waves.

"This is going to sound crazy," I said as we walked. "But I'm starting to worry that it wasn't Craig the other night."

"Who do you think it was?"

"I don't know. But I have this bad feeling they were after me."

His hand found mine and linked us together. "Explain."

"You know the barrette I lost, the one someone took off the cart the other day?"

He nodded.

"It was in my bedroom."

His steps faltered. "So you just misplaced it?"

"No. I had it at work that day. It's the only barrette I have like that. Someone took it… and then it turned up in my bedroom."

He stopped walking altogether and pulled me around so we were standing in the waves, facing each other.

"You think the person in your apartment the other night broke in to leave something there?"

"I know it sounds crazy."

His fingers tightened around mine. "I believe you."

"You do?"

"I'm on your side. I'll always believe you."

I don't know why, but tears pricked the backs of my eyes. I blinked furiously, trying to make them go away. Cam took my melting ice cream cone and put it inside his half-eaten waffle bowl, setting them both in the sand.

He pulled me into his arms, wrapping them both around me, holding me close and resting his chin atop my head. "Why didn't you say something sooner, sweetheart?"

"At first I thought I was just being irrational. But the more I think about it…"

"There's more?"

I nodded. He sighed and bent to pick up the now waterlogged ice cream and jogged over to throw it in a nearby trash can. Then we sat on the sand.

"Roxie took my car that night," I began. "She and I have similar looks… Both of us have long dark hair. We're both curvy…"

"What are you saying?"

"I'm saying what if someone was watching the house that night, waiting for me to come home? She pulled up in my car. From a distance and in the dark, someone could mistake her for me."

"Okay, I could see that," he said slowly. Tension began to radiate from his body and that's when I knew for sure I wasn't just being paranoid. This was a real possibility.

"But there's still that jerk Craig. He isn't exactly a boy scout." Cam continued.

"Roxie all but admitted that he was violent with her in the past."

"There is a possibility it was actually Craig, you know."

"Yeah, I know." I said it softly and the wind took my words and carried them away.

"But you're scared." His arm went around my waist, his fingers splaying out across my belly. He slid my body into his side and I leaned my head on his chest.

I sighed. I could sit like this—curled into his side—all day. "Maybe a little."

"It's okay to be scared," he told me. "It doesn't make you weak. It makes you smart."

"How does being scared make me smart?"

"Because it's your body and mind's way of protecting itself. Your brain is telling you something's wrong. Ignoring that feeling will only put you in danger and possibly cause you to miss things that could potentially save your life."

I tipped back my head. "You're a smart guy, Cam."

"I know."

I grinned. "So modest too."

"That's me, babe. Modest and smart and extremely good-looking."

"Did I say you were extremely good-looking?"

"You didn't have to. Your eyes say it all."

"You're okay I guess," I said playfully.

He let go of my waist and began feeling around my head.

"What are you doing?"

"Checking to see if that bump is still there. I think it damaged your mind when you fell."

"Ha. Ha."

He pressed a kiss to my forehead. "Want me to stay at your place tonight?"

I did. I knew I would feel better if he were there. "You don't have to do that. I'll be okay."

"I know I don't have to. I want to. Sleeping with you is a lot more exciting than sleeping alone."

"Do you sleep alone often?" I asked before I could cut off the urge to speak. "That's not really any of my business," I amended.

"I sleep alone every night I'm not with you."

It made me wonder who he slept with before we met, but thankfully I was able to contain that little gem of thought before I said it out loud.

We sat in silence for a long minute and I rested against his side, staring out over the endless blue ocean. "I've slept with other women before," he said softly. "I've dated a couple along the way."

I held my breath, wondering where this was going.

"Adam might not have been too far off when he said I was a player."

My stomach plummeted and I felt my body tense.

"But I swear I haven't thought about… I haven't even *looked* at another woman since you walked into the Mad Hatter and sat down in that freaking sexy sundress."

It certainly wasn't a declaration of love, but it was more than enough to make my heart skip a beat. "I'd really like if you stayed tonight. I would sleep better."

"You mean we have to sleep?" he purred, his hand moving up and covering my breast, giving it a gentle squeeze.

"That depends." I ran my hand up his arm still resting on my chest.

"On?"

"First one to the water gets to make the rules."

"We're not wearing bathing suits."

"Awww, Cam doesn't want to get his fancy board shorts wet." I braced myself, ready to run.

His eyes narrowed. I laughed and leapt up off the sand and raced toward the water.

Here's the thing: challenging an athletic guy who has legs almost two times longer than yours is stupid.

Unless of course you wanted to lose.

I didn't, however, mean to trip over my own feet and fall. Cam caught me around the waist and lifted me off my feet, carrying me into the water as I shrieked.

"I win. Now you have to do whatever I say."

"Darn," I said with mock disappointment.

"You played me."

"Like a fiddle," I sang.

He kept walking until he was waist deep in the ocean and past the point where the waves crested and then broke, rolling up to the shore. I was already wet when he placed my feet in the water and faced me.

"My turn to play you," he said.

"Bring it on, surfer dude," I teased, snagging the hat off his head and putting it on mine. Then I ran my hands through his blond hair, making it stand up all over.

He leaned down so the water lapped against his chest and reached for me, covering my mouth with his. He tasted sharp and salty like the water and his tongue was rough as it delved into my mouth. My fingers flexed against his T-shirt, which was plastered to his body, and my nails scraped across his back as his kiss deepened. My legs automatically wrapped around his waist, my core coming into direct contact with the bulge beneath his shorts.

A wave bounced us slightly, rocking us even closer, and we both groaned, kissing with a passionate fervor that literally stole my breath. When my lungs began to burn, I wrenched my mouth away and sucked in a lungful of blissful oxygen as we floated in the concealment of the sea.

He lifted his hips again, thrusting against me, and in response my hips bore down, rocking, as a little shudder ran up my spine. "We're in public," I moaned, leaning forward and sinking my teeth into his shoulder. One of my hands found its way between us and I gripped him, giving his hardness a squeeze and then rocking myself against him once more.

It was absolutely amazing to me how I could lose thought of everything when he touched me. All he had to do was kiss me and the floodgates of desire opened and I was swamped with the kind of need that was so powerful that I was actually in the center of the ocean, on a public beach, wishing there were no clothes between us and that he would slip himself inside me and rock me like the waves.

"No one can see what we're doing."

I groaned when he reached inside my shorts and flicked a finger over my clitoris. "I—" But my words fell away as an orgasm threatened to take over my body.

"Oh no you don't," he murmured, pulling his hand away.

I whimpered.

He unwound my legs and pulled me back, reaching between us and unfastening my shorts. I kicked up my legs, treading water as he slid them off and they floated up to the surface between us. The ocean water caressed my skin and heightened my arousal even more.

Then he did the same thing with my panties, except he wound them around his wrist like some kind of bracelet.

I was beyond thinking about what kind of fashion statement that was. I reached for his shorts, sliding them down his thighs and freeing his sex. My hand went to it, stroking it, the water making my hand glide over its thickness with impossible ease.

"Damn, baby."

"Have you ever done it in the ocean, Cam?" I purred, feeling emboldened by the desire written plainly across his face.

"No."

"Do you want to?"

He grabbed my face between his palms and yanked me forward kissing me senseless. I gripped onto his throbbing manhood and stroked it until the muscles in his stomach quivered.

He grabbed my hips and yanked me forward, my legs wrapping around his waist once more. I didn't even have to guide him to my entrance. It was like it remembered the way; it knew exactly where it belonged.

Just before he plunged into me, he swore and stiffened.

"What?" I gasped, wiggling a little against him.

His hands flexed at my hips. "I don't have any condoms."

"I'm on the pill." I'd been on it since I was seventeen and thought that my first time was going to be just weeks away. That didn't happen, but I continued taking it.

"You would let me…" His voice trailed away as his penis flexed, brushing against me.

I looked into his eyes. "I trust you, Cam."

"I've never done this with anyone else," he swore. "I've never done this bare."

"Do it," I ground out, shifting my hips so he slipped right inside.

A shudder passed through his entire body and moved into mine. His hold on me slipped and his eyes closed. I held a little tighter around his neck and we both just sat like that, the water pushing against us as he stretched me out fully.

He held me to him, his grip almost painful. His arms were like vices, holding me so tight that not even the water could come between us. He began to move—slow rocking motions that really only flexed him inside me because he didn't pull out but remained penetrated deeply inside.

He was so hard and so deep that he rubbed against the inside of my vaginal wall, and I suddenly understood all the talk about a G-spot. I was pretty sure that he managed to find it.

A few strings of curses slipped between his lips, sounding more like a prayer than bad language. "Is that...?" His voice was hoarse and he opened his eyes to look at me.

I nodded. "Please don't stop."

He laughed. "Sweetheart, I wouldn't even be able to stop if a shark came over here and ate my arm."

I moaned as the first wave of the orgasm washed over me. I fell against him, leaving him to support my weight completely. I couldn't do it. I couldn't hold myself up and experience the single most powerful thing to ever take over my body.

My mouth opened, but no sound came out.

It lasted longer than any other orgasm I'd ever felt. It seriously stripped away every single barrier that lay within me and bared me to him in a way that was far more intimate than being naked with our bodies joined together.

Emotion bubbled up in my chest until I thought it might burst. It was almost too intense. If I wasn't so caught up in the sensation of him, of his skin against my skin, I might have been embarrassed.

"Baby, I got to pull out," he murmured, his voice strained.

I made a sound of refusal, wrapping my arms tighter around him, not willing to let him go.

"Harlow, I can't hold it off much longer."

I found the energy to rock against him and then he came undone. I actually felt his hot seed pump into me, and it almost brought forward another climax.

I collapsed against him, laying my cheek on his shoulder, completely ignoring the water that would occasionally splash me directly in the face.

His arms were shaking, and we both sank a little lower into the ocean until just our heads were clear of the water.

Neither one of us said a word. There were no words that could possibly even come close to what we just experienced.

I'm pretty sure the little pieces of my heart he'd been collecting since the night we met were no longer just pieces. I'm pretty sure my heart had given itself over to him while our bodies were joined.

Part of me panicked; part of me wanted to snatch it back.

But the fact remained: I couldn't have it back. It was no longer mine.

Cam now held my heart in the palm of his hands. I wondered if he knew it. If he felt the shift between us while he made love to me. Because that was not sex. No sex could ever come close to that. I wondered if he felt powerful, if he realized the extent of the power he now held over me.

I wasn't about to ask.

I wasn't about to make him aware that he now had the total power to completely destroy me. Is this what love felt like? Did it strip a person so bare that it terrified them?

"Hey," Cam said gently, peeling me off his chest and holding me out to search my face. "That was intense. You okay?"

I nodded.

"I'm not going to hurt you," he vowed, almost like he could read my thoughts.

Or maybe his thoughts mirrored my own.

"I'm not going to hurt you either."

He gave me a lopsided smile. "You look good in my hat."

"I know."

"I think your shorts now belong to the sea."

There was no doubt in my mind. My heart belonged to Cam.

16

Cam was already behind the bar when I walked into the Mad Hatter. He was wearing his standard uniform of black pants, no shirt, and a bowtie. Tonight his hat was nowhere to be seen and his hair was still partially messy, which reminded me of the way I ran my fingers through it just a couple hours before.

The heat that flooded my limbs over the memory was momentarily cut off when a bimbo with her butt cheeks hanging out of her shorts and a top that probably was actually a bra leaned over the bar and grabbed Cam's hand.

"Hey there, gorgeous. I need a refill."

Cam smiled and reached for her glass. "No problem."

"I'll take your number too."

I wasn't a violent person, but in that split second, I thought about doing some bodily damage.

"Here's you drink," he said, handing over her glass. "On the house."

"What about your number?"

"I'm taken," he said and moved off down the bar. Her and her nasty butt cheeks stomped away.

Only then did I walk past the bar on my way backstage. Cam caught my eye and winked.

He knew I was watching.

I chuckled under my breath as I weaved through the crowd and backstage. Roxy was at her table, applying makeup to her eyes. "I heard from the cops," she said, lowering her voice.

"You did?" I leaned in, placing my elbows on her table.

Roxie nodded and then moved over to line her other eye as she spoke. "Apparently, Craig has an ironclad alibi for the other night."

"What kind of alibi?" An uncomfortable feeling clawed at my insides.

"Apparently he was out of town the night in question. That's why it took so long for the cops to bring him in. He just got back today."

"Convenient," I said, mulling over that information.

"That's what I said. But apparently he has several witnesses and a bunch of photos of him and the people he was with—including his new girlfriend."

I made a sound of disgust. "It never ceases to amaze me how dirt bags like him get women."

"It's the whole bad boy thing. Every woman thinks she wants one—until she actually has one. Then she can't run fast enough."

I guess I couldn't really say if that were true. My ex in high school was a jerk and spread rumors about me, but he wasn't really a bad boy. Since then, I pretty much avoided dating at all costs. It all seemed like too much trouble. Until I met Cam.

I wondered what the police were going to do now. What did it mean for our case if they eliminated the only suspect we had?

"Are you as tired as I am?" she asked wearily, setting down her makeup and looking at me.

"Yes. Cam said he was going to stay at our place tonight. Maybe we can get some sleep."

"Well, I will," she said, giving me the eye. I felt my cheeks flush and she laughed. "I don't know how you manage as a stripper, Violet. I really don't."

"Do you think Adam would just let me wait tables?" I asked, quieting my voice.

She pinned me with her purple stare. "You want to quit?"

I didn't know what I wanted. All I knew was the slightly queasy, nervous, shy part of me wasn't really going away. "I'm not sure. But I like working here."

"Usually the girls here have to dance."

"Yeah," I said. I knew that.

"Have that man of yours give you some sexy lessons," she called out as I walked to my table.

Oh, he'd given me some lessons. I already knew more about sex and pleasure than I ever thought I would. But that was part of the problem. I only wanted to share that part of myself with him. It seemed wrong somehow to give it to anyone else. Especially after today at the beach.

I took out one of my outfits (the one with the see-through purple stars) and the purple wig. I felt like I needed to really channel Violet tonight to get through the dancing.

I made it through the first couple of hours and dances okay. Whenever I felt like my nerve was slipping, my eyes would seek out Cam. We would lock eyes and I would pretend it was just him and me and my moves were for him.

I managed once again to not bare anything I didn't want to bare, but by the end of my second dance, some of the men in the back were yelling for me to take it all off.

I retreated off the stage without showing any of my… unmentionables. I wondered how long I could stall before Adam pulled me into his office and gave me the old heave-ho (aka, I get fired).

"Violet," Adam called, poking his head backstage just as I was heading to my dressing table.

I froze.

Seriously?

That was a lot faster than I thought it would be.

Geez, a couple drunken idiots start complaining and I'm out of a job.

"Yes?" I said, pivoting around to face him.

"My office. Now."

I felt like I was about to walk the plank. All the girls looked at me as I headed out the door to my doom.

"Adam," I said, walking in without knocking. "I can do bet—" I started to say, even while I wondered why I was bothering to lie.

"Someone's requesting a private dance."

"Excuse me?" I said, my previous sentence dying a swift and painless death.

"We got a guy out front that wants a private lap dance in the VIP room."

I'd never been in the VIP room. I knew it was there, sure. I'd seen the girls go in and out on a nightly basis. I never asked what went on in there, but I knew it was more risqué than the stage… If it wasn't, there wouldn't be a need for a private room.

"I haven't… I mean… I don't know what to do," I said miserably.

He sighed heavily and sat down behind his desk. "I told him no at first. I figured you weren't ready. But he was persistent. And then he gave me a number. I figured I would give you the option."

A number? An option? "You aren't going to make me?"

"Hell no," he said. "I may own a strip club, I may make money off girls shaking their tits and showing some skin, but I respect women."

I don't know why, but I laughed.

He glared at me and the sound died on my lips. "I'm sorry."

He grinned. "Please. You don't think I know how I look? What everyone thinks of me?" He sat back in his leather chair and wiped a hand over the top of his ultra-short hair.

"I may not be a choir boy. Hell, I may have never stepped foot in a church. But I don't force women. The girls that work for me get better hourly pay than any other strip joint down here. I've got bouncers that know the girls come first, and I enforce a strict no-touching policy. You girls don't have to do anything you don't feel comfortable with, and I think you know that." He glared directly at my boobs. "If I were anyone else, you'd already be fired."

"About that—" I said nervously.

He held up a hand. "We'll talk about it later." He looked up, studying me with blue eyes. I never really noticed how blue they were before. "I like you. Roxie likes you. You've been good to her. You convinced her to move out and live with you." He paused. "And somehow you've managed to catch and hold the eye of a guy I've never seen with the same girl more than a handful of times."

"Says the man on wife number four," I muttered, not really caring for his insult of Cam.

He laughed. "Didn't you hear? She moved out."

I rolled my eyes. But that was interesting news… I wondered what that meant for him and Roxie. "I can't imagine why. You're such a charmer."

"Two thousand."

"What?" I said, not following the quick change of conversation.

"He offered to pay you two grand for fifteen minutes in the VIP room."

My mouth opened. It closed. It fell open again. "Is that normal?"

"I've seen some girls walk outta there with a hefty wad of cash, but never that much."

"I don't understand."

"I'm thinking that little hard-to-get act you got going on the stage has made someone real curious about what's underneath those clothes."

"Like they leave anything to the imagination," I muttered.

"Someone's got two grand that says they do."

That was a lot of money. Like *a lot*. That would almost pay for an entire semester of school. I'd be a fool to turn that down. "What will I have to do?"

"Nothing you don't want to do."

"But what will he expect?" Surely that amount of money demanded certain things.

"A lap dance. Basically standing over him, shaking it. You're going to have to lose your top. I hope you got a thong because that wouldn't hurt."

I chewed my lower lip while I weighed my options.

"You can touch him." Adam continued. "But the same club rules apply. He cannot under any circumstances touch you."

"He can look, but he can't touch," I murmured.

"Exactly."

Part of me wondered what Cam would say about me going into a private room with another man where I was expected to take off my clothes. But this wasn't about Cam. It was about me. My willingness to do this and my need for the money.

If I did this one job, I could stop stripping altogether. I could get another job waiting tables. Fifteen minutes of my life for an entire semester of school without stress.

"I'll do it."

Adam seemed surprised. "You're sure?"

I nodded. "I need that money."

He studied me. "You in some kind of trouble?"

"What? No. Nothing like that. I lost my financial aid for school, and if I don't come up with the money, I'm going to have to drop out and move home."

"How much college you have left?"

"Two years."

"All right. I'll tell him you'll do it. I'm going to put Ty at the door. If he even breathes on you funny, you yell for him."

I nodded and headed for the door.

"Violet," he called.

I looked over my shoulder.

"Even if you yell for help, you still get paid. The minute he walks into that VIP room, that money is yours."

"What's your cut?"

"None. It's all yours."

Now I understood why some of the girls always wanted to go to the VIP room.

"How long do I have?"

"Go change, do whatever you need to do, and then get to the room. He'll be waiting. When your fifteen minutes are up, Ty will tell you."

I walked out of his office and my eyes went straight to the bar. Cam was watching the door. He looked a little more subdued than usual. I gave him all the smile I could muster and then turned and fled backstage.

I was a coward.

I didn't want to see the disappointment or the hurt on his face by what I was about to do.

I stared down at my outfits, trying to decide what to wear. Suddenly I wondered what the hell I'd been thinking choosing any of it. It was all tiny. It wouldn't take long at all to remove.

I decided on the hot-pink bodice with the black satin laces up the front and the tiny black boy shorts with the pink skulls. Maybe I could take my time untying the lace and waste time.

I put it all on, added my black stilettos, and then sat at the mirror, trying to calm my nerves. I lifted my eyeliner but couldn't apply it because my hand was trembling.

Why would someone—anyone—pay that much money to see me dance? It was beyond ridiculous. Didn't he have better things to buy? He was probably some colossal nerd who couldn't get a date. Or maybe he was some pervert who wanted to stare at me while he jerked off.

I was going to be sick.

I lurched up off the chair and stood there like a startled deer in a pair of headlights.

"Whoa, there," Roxie said, coming up beside me. "Did he fire you?" she demanded. "I will kick his ass."

"No," I said, taking a deep breath. "I'm supposed to go to the VIP room."

"How long?"

"Fifteen minutes."

"That's manageable," she said, pushing me down into the chair again. She picked up a brush and began to style my hair. I let her because I was too busy freaking out.

"Make sure you bend over right in his face. Men are such pigs. They get off on that."

I nodded.

"And touch yourself. You can do that from across the room so you don't have to be so close to him. Touch yourself and then touch him. They love that."

Ew.

"How can you stand it?" I whispered.

The brush paused halfway through my hair. "I shut my mind off and don't think about it. Or I think about someone I would actually like to dance for."

"Who is that for you?" I wondered, knowing for me it was Cam.

"Adam," she said matter-of-factly.

"His wife moved out."

She glanced at me through the mirror. "I heard."

She finished with my hair and then patted my shoulder. "You're done."

My hair was waving around my shoulders and the purple pop of color accentuated my eyes. "Here I go." I got up, adjusting my outfit.

"I'll see you in a few," she said.

Cam was standing on the other side of the door when I opened it and walked through.

His eyes swept over me. "You're doing it."

"It's two thousand dollars."

His eyes widened. "Shit."

I nodded.

"I brought you something." He held out a shot glass full of vodka.

I didn't hesitate to down it in one gulp. It burned the whole way down. "Thanks."

He moved so fast I didn't see it coming. One minute he was across the hall and the next he was pinning me against the wall with his body. His lips covered mine in an aggressive kiss that set fire to my blood.

It was over too fast and he spun away, breathing hard.

He was angry.

I didn't blame him.

I held a hand up to my bruised lips and stared at his back as his shoulders rose and fell.

"I'm sorry," I whispered, then moved off down the hall. Just before I turned the corner, he was on me again, pulling me back so my back was against his chest and I couldn't see his face. But I could hear his voice just fine.

"Remember that kiss when you're dancing for him. Don't see him; see me. And when you come out of that room, I want you to be ready."

"Be ready?" I said, my voice trembling.

"Be ready because I'm going to make love to you all night long until the only thing you feel is me and you don't even remember his face."

"Oh, Cam," I sighed. "You already are the only man I see."

He pulled away, going back to the bar and leaving me shaking in the darkened hallway. As I straightened and walked toward the elusive VIP room, I wondered if Cam would still want me when I came out.

17

He was sitting in the shadows.

The room was a small square with black velvet walls, a silver pole that ran from ceiling to floor near the center, and the wall farthest from me was covered with a giant mirror all the way down to the long bed that was draped in fabric and pillows.

A chandelier hung from the center of the ceiling and it cast dim lighting mostly right beneath it and a shadowed glow around the rest of the room.

Ty stood at the door and he inclined his chin, whispering that he would be right there as I went past. I was a little surprised that he didn't close the door behind me but lowered a black velvet curtain across the opening. I could see his booted feet at the bottom, and I was glad he was right there.

The man sat in a straight-backed chair, which wasn't beneath the light of the chandelier. Instead, it was pushed back into the shadowed perimeter of the room.

He wore jeans and dark-colored shoes and a dark top. He had a baseball cap on his head and my heart gave a little squeeze because it reminded me of Cam. At least it wasn't on backward. That may have sent me fleeing from the room.

His hands were at his sides and he sat still, but I could feel his eyes on me as I moved across the room.

"I'm Violet," I said, keeping my voice low. "You requested my presence and I came."

Sexy music began pumping over the speakers into the room and I knew my fifteen minutes had begun.

I can do this.

I started at the pole, moving around it, wrapping my leg around it, gyrating against it. Then I moved over to the wall, leaning against it and spreading my legs wide. I squatted down, running my hands up my legs and to the inside of my thighs. Then I pushed up, turning around, keeping my legs spread, and bent over. I felt the little boy shorts ride up my butt, and I couldn't help but wonder if he enjoyed the view.

After a few minutes, I walked over to him, strutting, swaying my hips, and straddling his lap—still standing—and pressed my chest near his face. Then I stepped back, still in front of him, and reached for the bow at the bottom of the corset.

Slowly, I untied the laces, keeping my feet planted to the floor. I heard some commotion out in the bar and glanced over my shoulder briefly, wondering what was going on.

But then I brushed it off and turned back, still untying the top.

I heard another sound and I looked back at the curtain, noting that Ty's feet were no longer visible.

Where had he gone?

"Get on the bed," the man spoke, his voice startling me. I looked directly at his face, but I was unable to make out any kind of features. It was dark and the brim of the hat made it even harder to see him.

I stepped toward the bed, making a big production of climbing across it, keeping my bum in view.

"Lay down," the man instructed. His voice sounded extraordinarily deep, almost like he was trying to disguise it.

Maybe he didn't want anyone to know he was here.

I lay down like he asked, looking again for Ty. He still wasn't there.

"Untie your top. All the way."

I finished untying it but didn't pull it open. My heart pounded so heavily that I barely heard his next command.

"Spread your legs."

This was weird. Is this the way it was supposed to be?

I hesitated. The man stood. "I said spread your legs."

I listened, hoping he would sit back down.

He didn't. He prowled closer, looming over me and staring down.

"Open your top and touch yourself."

I couldn't do this. I couldn't. I would just give him all his money back and then I was going to quit.

I heard a bunch of shouting out front and the sound of glass shattering.

I stiffened and prepared to stand up to flee, but the stranger took advantage of my preoccupation.

He pounced on me, pinning me on the bed and making me cry out.

"No touching!" I insisted.

He laughed.

"Ty!" I screamed.

But Ty wasn't there.

The man leaned down. "You're nothing but a little *tease*," he spat.

Something about his words bothered me. They struck a chord deep within. "Get. Off." I growled.

He put a hand over my mouth, silencing me. I began to panic. I tried to buck him off. That was a huge mistake because all my struggling seemed to arouse him. The bulge in his pants grew and grew until it was all I could stare at.

Tears filled my eyes and I shook my head no.

He shook his head yes.

"Don't scream," he ordered low. "Or I'll make it hurt."

Oh. My. God.

He pulled his hand away to part the corset covering my chest. I belted out an ear-piercing scream and struggled anew.

"You stupid bitch," he roared and backhanded me across the face.

I saw stars. Then I felt the air brush against my naked chest.

"Harlow!" someone roared, and then the stranger was gone and this sick thudding sound filled my ears.

I scrambled off the bed, staring across the room.

Cam was beating the man, ramming his fist into his face over and over again.

"Cam!" I cried. His fist stopped in midair and he dropped the man to the floor. His eyes took in my rumpled appearance and partially exposed chest.

He crossed the room in two great strides, pulling the corset around me and then tucking me against his chest. I couldn't help but cry. I was humiliated. I was hurt. I was violated.

There was a groan and Cam stiffened. He tried to pull away, but I clutched at him. "It's okay," he murmured, his arms coming around me once more.

I glanced up just as the stranger pulled back a curtain that was behind his chair to reveal an emergency exit. He shoved open the door and raced out into the night.

Cam moved to go after him.

"No!" I cried. "Let him go." I wouldn't be able to take it if Cam got hurt trying to protect me.

"Fuck!" he yelled to no one in particular.

He looked down at my face, touched where the skin burned and stung, and he cussed again when I winced. "Come on," he said, taking my hand and towing me out behind the bar. He grabbed his black leather jacket and held it out. I slipped my arms inside. It smelled like the beach, like him.

He zipped it up around my body, covering me and then he leaned forward and kissed my forehead. I wanted to cry all over again. Then he filled a plastic baggy with ice from the ice machine, wrapped it in his T-shirt, and then ever so easily held it to my face.

"Where else did he hurt you?"

More shattering glass had me looking out into the bar where I suddenly understood why Ty had disappeared. A massive bar fight had broken out. Beer bottles were flying, people were punching and yelling, and one guy was wielding a chair.

The bouncers were pulling people apart and flinging them toward the door. I heard Roxie scream and I called out her name, rushing toward the fight.

"No you don't," Cam said, pulling me back.

"Roxie," I told him.

"She's fine." He pointed.

She was in the center of it all, but Adam stood beside her, and anyone that came close got disposed of rather easily.

"What's going on?"

"Craig," Cam spat, like that explained it all.

"I thought the police cleared him."

"Well, he was awful pissed off, showing up and yelling at Roxie for having him arrested by the cops. He lunged for her. Someone intercepted him. The result was a massive bar fight, a huge mess, and you being left alone in the VIP room with a fucking attempted rapist."

His words left me cold. Like I had ice water running through my veins. I glanced back toward Roxie, who was making her way across the empty stage with Adam at her back, shielding her body with his. When she disappeared backstage, Adam reappeared and gave a signal to the DJ.

The music cut off and the DJ came over the speakers. "The Mad Hatter is now closed. Get the hell out before the cops get here to haul you away."

For the most part, the fighting stopped. What little continued, the bouncers took care of in short notice and tossed the men out into the parking lot. I wondered where my attacker was, if he was still out there lurking.

As the crowd thinned, I noticed a guy, with longish dark hair and a sleeve of tattoos up his right arm, sprawled across the floor. Adam stood over his body, crossing his arms over his chest and glaring down.

Police sirens sounded in the distance and I was grateful they were almost here.

Before the cops arrived on the scene, Adam drew back his large booted foot and kicked the man in the ribs. He groaned.

I figured it was Craig.

Adam seemed to sense us staring and he looked at me, his gaze sharpening. "What the hell happened to you?"

I opened my mouth to tell him I was fine, but Cam spoke over me. "Fucking pervert tried to rape her."

Adam's body jerked like he was shot. I tried not to listen to the words that flung out of his mouth like swords. I wondered where he learned words like that.

The police arrived, escorted Craig to the back of a cop car, and interviewed all the people who were still lingering and had information.

Roxie looked like a Mack truck ran her over by the time she told the cops about how Craig had burst in there tonight and tried to start a fight and do her physical harm. She was pressing charges and if those didn't stick, she was getting a restraining order. I hoped Craig was looking at jail time.

Roxie didn't seem as relieved as me, but I figured once the shock wore off she would be.

Then it was my turn to talk to the police. I couldn't give them a very good description of the man who attacked me because I never actually saw his face clearly. All I saw were flashes of a strong jaw, stubble, and lips that might have been nice if they weren't spewing out sick words. As I talked, I realized… there was something about him that was vaguely familiar. Something that I didn't catch right away because I'd been so scared and freaked out.

What's more was the scent of his cologne lingered on me… wrapping around my senses and invading my feeling of relief that he was gone. It was an older scent, something that had been out for several years, a popular men's brand. I knew it well because it came out while I was still in high school, and I swear every guy at school went out and bought it. The hallways smelled just like it the entire year.

The police kept asking questions, and I repeated what happened, the exact words he said, and what I was feeling/doing while he said them. Cam remained eerily silent through my story and that gave me a queasy feeling in the pit of my stomach.

When I was done talking, the only thing he said was directed at the police. "When are you going to catch this rapist?"

"He didn't rape me." Why did he keep saying that? It was making me sick. And really, I didn't know if he planned to rape me or not. I really hadn't known at all what he was going to do. Although, whatever it was, it wasn't good.

"We're going to do everything we can to catch this guy. If you see him or think he might be close by, please call 9-1-1 immediately," the officer replied in a no-nonsense tone.

"Let's go," Cam said, placing his hand on the small of my back.

"Shouldn't we stay? Help clean up?"

Adam overheard and approached, his feet crunching over broken glass as he walked. "I'll just call in the cleaning service I use. I'll get them here tomorrow morning and then we'll open up at four tomorrow evening. Business as usual."

I took a breath. "I'm going to have to give my notice. I'm just not cut out to be a stripper. I can stay on until you find a replacement but, I—I don't think I can dance anymore."

Adam held up a hand. "You're not quitting."

When I opened my mouth to protest, he just kept right on talking. Like a train on a track, he sped over my words.

"You don't have to dance. You can just wait tables."

"Really?"

He nodded. "But you're going to have to wear skimpy clothes while you do it. Can you handle that?"

I nodded. "Definitely."

"Good. I'm sorry about what happened tonight. Ty should have been there at the door. That shouldn't have happened."

"It's okay. I'm sure Ty was just trying to help out here."

Adam's lips drew into a thin line. "That asshole even so much as steps foot in the parking lot of this place and he's going to wish he was still in jail."

"Which one?" I asked, wondering if we were talking about my attacker or Roxie's.

"Both of them," Adam and Cam answered at the exact same time.

The testosterone in here was getting a bit thick.

"So is it okay for me to leave, then?" I asked Adam, deciding that a change of subject was probably best. Roxie approached as I spoke, looking as tired as I felt.

"Of course. If you don't feel up to coming in tomorrow night, just call. I understand. You went through a lot tonight."

"What happened!" Roxie gasped. "Did you get caught up in the fight?"

I shot Cam a glare, just daring him to use the R word again. He seemed to get my message and kept his mouth shut. "I was in the VIP room. Things didn't go well."

"What do you mean?" she said, taking in my appearance and the fact I was wearing Cam's jacket over my clothes.

"I'll explain later."

She nodded.

I glanced at Cam. "Are you still staying at our place?" I asked, wondering if he changed his mind.

"Definitely," he replied.

"Thank God," Roxie muttered, mirroring my own thoughts exactly. "I feel like the walking dead."

"Why didn't you tell me you couldn't sleep?" Adam said, looking at Roxie with genuine concern.

"Because it's not your problem."

His lips thinned again. "I'll drive you home. And then I'm sleeping on the couch."

I thought she might argue, but she didn't. Instead, she nodded and went over to the bar and sat down. I went into the back to grab my duffle, too tired to bother changing, instead just leaving Cam's jacket over my outfit. Cam stood in the doorway and watched me like he was afraid to let me out of his sight.

On the way to the door, Adam called my name and strode across the room, extending a white envelope to me. "What's this?"

"It's your two grand."

I looked at the envelope like it was a rattlesnake. "You don't have to pay me that."

He snorted. "He paid it before he went into the VIP room. This money is yours. I know it doesn't make up for what happened, but I know you could use it."

I swallowed, reaching out and taking the money. "Thank you," I murmured, stuffing the envelope into my bag. It felt like blood money. I felt dirty accepting it. But he was right; I did need it, especially now that I wasn't going to be stripping anymore.

I drove home, leaving the radio off, not needing the added noise to my already loud thoughts. Cam followed close behind on his bike, almost as if I were some celebrity with a police escort or a bodyguard.

What a freaking mess everything was.

First someone steals my barrette; then someone forces himself into my apartment, attacks Roxie, but leaves behind my barrette. Then Craig bursts into the club, angry about being accused of something he probably thought about doing, and tried to attack Roxie. Meanwhile, I was in the back giving a freaking striptease to a man who… well… It did seem like he wanted to rape me.

But why?

I mean, I guess I got *why* a man would rape a woman. But in the middle of a club? And everything that happened before led me to believe this guy might have been watching me for a while.

I shivered, fear clawing its way up my spine and squeezing my chest.

Cam's headlight in the rearview mirror caught my eye. *Cam.* He was always so chill, so calm and easy. He rocked that "surfer dude" stereotype like no one else I'd ever met… but tonight I'd seen a different side of him. The steely core beneath his easygoing exterior. He was angry—beyond angry—and the way he looked at me… It made me wonder if he decided maybe I wasn't worth all the trouble that seemed to rain down upon us.

And yeah… maybe part of me—a very small part—wondered. Wondered if maybe he was so attracted to me because up until him, I had basically been untouched. Yes, I made out with guys before. Yes, I did things… sexy things… But what Cam and I had? What we shared? He was my one. He was my only. I knew he liked that. What guy wouldn't?

Except now I was tainted.

I was soiled.

Someone else touched me. Grabbed me. Talked dirty to me.

The memory of the man on top of me, telling me I was nothing but a tease, came over me. A car horn blared loudly and I snapped out of it just in time to see the overly bright headlights of an oncoming car as it barreled straight at me.

18

I jerked the wheel, swerving back into my lane, narrowly avoiding an accident.

I drove the rest of the way with a pounding heart, gripping the steering wheel until my knuckles ached. Finally, I pulled into the parking lot of my apartment and let out a huge sigh of relief.

Cam was parked and off his bike in lightning speed. He pulled open the car door and leaned down just as I shut off the engine.

"Are you okay?" he demanded. "What the hell was that?" He ran a hand through his hair and then stared at me. "Are you sure you aren't hurt? You'd tell me if you were hurt, right?"

"Yes, I'd tell you. I'm not hurt."

He stepped back for me to get out and then reached into the back to grab my bag. I walked ahead of him up the stairs and unlocked the door, pushing it open. Cam shouldered by me, going in first and flipping on the lights. He went through the apartment while I went into the kitchen to grab a bottle of water.

The icy coolness of the drink felt wonderful against my throat.

"Everything looks fine," he said, coming into the kitchen and grabbing a beer out of the fridge (I finally bought some man food).

"I'm going to take a shower."

He nodded. I felt his eyes follow me as I walked out of the room. He didn't say anything. I didn't say anything.

For some reason the silence hurt.

In the bathroom, I unzipped his leather jacket and peeled it away, taking care to hang it on the back of the door. Then I stared at myself in the mirror. The pink corset was still untied. The lace ribbon was rumpled and wrinkled. It hung open just enough so I could see a gap of skin, from my neck all the way down below my navel.

My hair was tangled in dark waves around my shoulders and cheeks. My skin was pale and my eyes were red. I spun away from the mirror and reached into the shower to start the water, turning it the hottest it would go.

I stepped out of my heels and pulled off the boy shorts, kicking them into the corner where I hoped I never had to see them again. Then I reached for the corset.

Open your top and touch yourself.

The words—*his words*—echoed through my head a million times, bouncing off every barrier they hit until I couldn't take it anymore.

I ripped the corset off my body, balling it up into a tiny wad of fabric and then throwing it against the wall. My chest was heaving when I glanced back in the mirror. Even through the shroud of tears, my blurred vision saw it.

The bruise.

There was a bruise on my left breast—marks from where his hand had grabbed me, where his fingers brutalized my flesh. I hadn't even felt it. Why hadn't I felt him grab me?

It must have been just before Cam pulled him off.

I stared at the discolored patches on my otherwise creamy breast. *Fingerprints.* I had the fingerprints of a… a *rapist* on my body.

A sob so deep ripped through my body, causing me to double over the sink. I sat there for long minutes just breathing, and then I pushed away and stepped behind the curtain and beneath the scalding hot water.

It burned. It made my skin tingle and turn a blotchy red. But I didn't care. I wanted him off me. I wanted every last trace of that sick human being to wash down the drain so I never had to feel like this again.

I grabbed up the soap and started at my shoulder, gripping the bar so hard that my fingers turned white and the soap bore the indent of my hand. I covered my arm in a thick lather, trying to wash away everything.

But you can't wash away a memory.

The soap slipped out of my hand and hit the floor of the shower with a loud bang. I stood under the too-hot water and started to cry. The sobs were so deep I didn't even breathe. All I could do was heave as big fat tears rolled down my cheeks and mixed with the water of the shower. I cried silently—the kind of cry that was so painful my body just wasn't capable of making noise.

I was mad at myself. Mad for putting myself in that position. Mad for not listening to my gut and trying to hold on to a job I really didn't want. Mad that I felt dirty and used. Mad that every time I looked at my chest and saw that bruise, I was going to be reminded.

I leaned against the shower wall, resting my forehead against the tile and sucking in great gulps of oxygen.

The shower curtain slid open and Cam stepped into the shower, pulling the curtain closed behind him.

"Hey," he murmured, lifting his hand but letting it fall between us.

He didn't want to touch me.

A sob echoed around me. And then another. I couldn't even remember the last time I cried this hard.

"Don't cry," he said, his voice breaking just a little. His body shifted closer.

He was wearing all his clothes. Even his shoes.

"I'm stained now, aren't I?" I said, my voice hollow and deep.

"What?"

"It's the reason you don't want to touch me. It's because of him. Because he touched me."

He made a sound like he was in pain. "Is that what you think? You think I don't want to touch you now?"

I didn't reply. I just let the water pour over my back and kept my forehead against the wall.

"I'm afraid to touch you. I'm afraid if I do that, you'll flinch away. If you flinch, I'll hunt him down and kill him."

"I'm not going to flinch."

He hauled me against him, wrapping me up against his body and holding my head to his chest. I could feel the hard beating of his heart and the finest of tremors through his arms.

"Your skin is burning up," he said, turning so the water hit him in the back and I was no longer underneath the spray.

"I want him off me."

Cam bent and picked up the soap and used it to gently wash my skin. I shook my head. "Harder, it needs to be harder."

He pressed a little harder, covering me in bubbles and then using his hands to rinse them away. I knew immediately when he saw the marks. He stilled. He didn't breathe as he discarded the soap.

He traced his fingers over the fingerprints of another man. Then he leaned down and kissed them softly. Tears clogged my throat because his tenderness was utterly sweet. "I'm so sorry, baby," he whispered and pulled me into him, hugging me close.

The water eventually cooled, and I pulled away to wash my hair as he stood there in dripping wet clothes and watched me with hooded eyes. I couldn't really decipher his expression and I was partially glad for it.

My skin was still splotchy and red when I shut off the water, and Cam wrapped a giant towel around my body. He ran his hands up and down my arms, drying as he went. Once I was dry, I combed out my hair and put some moisturizer on my skin.

"You're dripping all over the floor," I observed.

"I'll change when you're finished."

"Why not now?"

"I wasn't sure if you'd want to see me naked."

"Why?"

He let out a breath. "Because of what happened. I have no idea what you need."

I turned and leaned against the sink, pinning him with a stare. "Why don't you ask me?"

"What do you need, Harlow?"

"Don't treat me like I'm broken. Don't tiptoe around because you think you might scare me or make me think of something bad. I'm already scared. My thoughts are already dark. But I'm not broken Cam." I reached up and opened the towel wrapped around my body, letting it drift to the floor. "I'm safe in your arms. I don't think at all when I'm in your arms. Make it go away. Erase everything he did to me with the power of your touch."

"Are you sure that's what you want? I don't expect you—"

"It's what I want."

His eyes traveled over my naked body, turning into molten chocolate sauce. "Wait here," he murmured and brushed past me, disappearing out the bathroom door.

Not exactly the reaction I was hoping for.

I used the towel to wipe up the puddles on the floor and then hung it up as the door opened and Cam stood in the frame. He wasn't wearing his wet clothes anymore. He was wearing a pair of basketball shorts and nothing else. His hair was damp and disheveled, falling across his forehead.

"Roxie and Adam aren't here yet," he said and then swept me up into his arms, cradling me against his chest, and walked back through the apartment, using his foot to push the bedroom door open and then moving inside. He laid me across the bed, which had already been turned down, and then went to shut the door and lock it.

Delicious anticipation began in my toes and climbed up me like a vine growing in a field.

He prowled over to the side of the bed. He made me feel hunted—but he was the kind of hunter you would lie down just to let him catch you. He was the kind of killer that you would beg to kill you just so he would put his hands any place on your skin.

"This isn't going to be like the other times," he said, his voice low. "This isn't going to be aggressive; this isn't going to be in a public place."

He lay down beside me, stretching out along my side. His hand hovered over me. I could feel the heat in his palm. I wanted him to touch me—I *needed* him to—but still he resisted.

"It's just me and you right now. I'm going to take my time with you tonight. I'm going to touch you gently, not because I think you're broken, but because to me you're something to be cherished. And because the only way to completely chase away the dark from your mind is to fill you up so completely with light that the darkness has nowhere to hide."

If words could give a girl an orgasm, those words would totally do it.

"If you change your mind, all you have to say is stop. I'll stop. I won't leave, and I won't be mad."

I wasn't going to ask him to stop.

I ran my hand through his hair, loving the way the thick strands curled around my fingers, and then spread out my fingers, cupping the back of his neck and pulling his head down.

His lips had their own idea.

Instead of meeting my mouth, he ran his tongue over the nipple closest to him, swirling over the top like I was some kind of ice cream cone and he was hungry for a snack. My back arched upward and he tucked his arm between me and the mattress, supporting my weight and lifting me farther off the bed and into his hungry and waiting mouth.

He licked me with slow, deliberate strokes, suckling parts of my flesh into his mouth, gently tugging and igniting all my senses. His teeth lightly grazed over one nipple and then the other, and then he pressed soft and tender kisses in the center of my breasts. His mouth trailed downward, across my belly, kissing around my navel and flirting with the short curls just above my core.

His arm slid out from under me and I lowered to the bed. He rose over me, completely blocking everything else from sight. I was shivering lightly, likely from passion, but he pulled the covers up over us both, further cocooning us together, the weight of the blankets pressing our skin just a little bit closer.

Cam moved over me, kissing every inch. I noticed the way his skin was a different texture than mine. He felt coarser, not quite as smooth, while mine was like silk that glided right across his roughness.

Careful to keep his weight off of me, he lowered only enough that his barely there touch drove me mad. His hands and fingers never stopped; he found places on my body that I hadn't even discovered.

There was a spot behind my ear that whenever he kissed it, I purred. There were three freckles on the side of my right breast—I knew that's how many there were because Cam whispered as he counted them.

He kissed my eyelids, my nose, and all the places in between, but he had yet to kiss my lips.

Cam disappeared beneath the blanket, slowly looping my legs around his neck and settling between my thighs like there was no place he would rather be.

I knew there wasn't. Because he whispered that too.

His tongue was thorough and undemanding as he explored the folds, gently suckling them with his mouth and then smoothing it over with his tongue. He teased my clit by pulling it into his mouth and flicking his tongue over it, and when my body would begin to shudder, he would pull back and repeat the whole thing over again.

It was torture at its sweetest.

It was prolonged agony at its best.

I was so saturated with want for him that the insides of my thighs were moist with my juices. He licked that too. Two fingers slipped into my entrance, delving inside me with easy grace. He moved them this way and that way, leaning down to take the swollen bud into his mouth to suckle some more.

A delicious pressure began to build. My body felt heavy with it, but it was far from uncomfortable. Then he slipped his fingers out of me and reached up, swirling his damp fingers over my nipple, drawing it into a fine point.

I moaned.

He slid up my body, taking the very same nipple into his mouth and then finally coming up and lowering his mouth to mine. He tasted slightly different, and I knew what I tasted was me on his lips. I licked into his mouth, wanting more, wanting at least part of me to be inside him. I rocked up my hips, searching for what I wanted, trying to tell him without saying a word.

He rose onto his knees between my thighs and grabbed a condom from beneath a nearby pillow. I watched him roll it on. It stretched across his incredible girth and I had the urge to take him into my mouth and lick him until he spilled across my tongue.

He seemed to know what I was thinking because he shook his head and then came back over me, pressing a feather-light kiss to my lips.

In one even stroke, he was inside me, my insides tightening around him like they might never let go. I stretched against him like a cat, lifting my arms above my head and baring my chest to his hungry mouth.

We moved against each other. We moved as one as his lips explored my chest and my lips whispered his name. He raised up onto his hands, poised above me, and looked down.

"I've never felt anything like this before," he confided.

"Neither have I."

We began to move again until the pressure became unbearable and my hips started to grind against his. I splintered apart, shattering into a million tiny pieces, knowing when the pieces came back together, I wasn't going to be the same as before.

My name ripped from his lips, sounding like a groan, as his release rippled through him, causing his head to fall back and a moan to float up above us into the ceiling.

He grasped me around the waist and rolled, keeping himself firmly planted inside me and taking all my weight so I was lying directly on top of him with my legs spread on either side, his sex still twitching inside me.

"I think I love you," he whispered. "No. I don't think. I know." He brushed the hair back away from my face. "I'm so in love with you it scares me."

"I love you too."

He grasped my face in his palms. "People are going to say it's too soon. That what's between us is only lust."

"Sometimes people suck."

He chuckled. "Yeah, they do."

"I don't care what other people think. I only care what you think. And you know what's in here." I placed his hand over my chest. "You know what it feels like when our eyes meet across the room, or when you're inside me and it's not just our bodies that are connected."

"Fuck 'em," he said.

"Fuck 'em all." I agreed.

I pressed my cheek against his chest and we lay there quietly while he trailed his fingers along my spine.

"Why did you apply for the job at the Mad Hatter?"

"Because I lost some of my tuition assistance for school. My roommate graduated and moved out, and

I was left wondering how I was going to keep up with rent and pay for school."

"Why'd you lose your tuition assistance? Did you get bad grades?"

I laughed and poked him in the ribs. "No. I did not get bad grades. I don't really know why. Government cuts? School cuts? Who knows? All I know is the money I need isn't there."

"So you became a stripper."

I snorted. "The worst stripper ever."

"I could never keep my eyes off you."

"Whenever I got really nervous or sucked really bad, I would look at you," I whispered, a small secret smile playing on my lips.

"I'm glad you quit."

I lifted my head, surprised. "You are?"

"The thought of anyone seeing you…" He cupped my bare butt cheek. "…seeing the places only I've seen, drives me insane."

"It does?"

He smiled, the dimple appearing on his cheek. I kissed it. "I could barely see straight when you went back into that VIP room."

"Why didn't you say something?" I asked, propping my chin on his chest and gazing at him.

"It's not my job to tell you what to do."

"Then what is your job?" I said, arching a brow.

"To tell you that you're beautiful. To kiss you. To love you." He spoke softly, tucking a strand of hair behind my ear.

My belly did a little flop with the combination of his words and his touch. "Mmmm. You're an overachiever."

"So are you." His lips curved up in a smile.

I heard the front door open and close. My body stiffened and my breathing came in shallow pants. "It's Roxie," I murmured.

We listened to the sounds in the living room. Someone bumped into something and I cringed.

"I'm going to go make sure it's them."

"You don't have to do that."

He lifted me off him, depositing me on a pillow and tucking the blankets around me. "If I don't, you'll worry all night."

He got up and pulled on a pair of shorts and disappeared. I heard a few quiet voices and then the bathroom sink ran and the toilet flushed. Then he was talking again, his voice seeming farther away than before.

Minutes later, he came back in the room with a bottle of water that he handed to me. I sat up and took a sip.

"It's just Roxie and Adam. Adam's making up the couch."

"How's Roxie?"

"She seemed okay."

That was such a guy answer. He probably wouldn't know how she was unless she was sobbing or laughing. I would just see for myself tomorrow. Adam was with her and I could tell he cared about her a lot, even if neither one of them was willing to admit it.

I lifted the covers on the bed in invitation to Cam. He smiled and slid between them, taking me in his arms and shutting off the light.

"Go to sleep, baby. Nothing is going to bother you tonight."

I was exhausted and he was so incredibly warm and comfortable that I drifted off just as I was thinking sleep would likely be elusive.

And when I jolted awake in the deep of the night, my heart pounding and fear rearing its ugly head, I reached for Cam. He was there.

I felt better.

19

The gentle caress of his lips stirred me awake and I opened one eye to peer at him through the very early, very dim light of a new day. His head was resting right beside mine, and he watched me with a small smile on his face.

"What?" I said, my voice slightly slurred and thick from sleep.

He chuckled. Even I couldn't be grouchy when he sounded so pleased. "I'm supposed to give a surf lesson at the beach in a bit. Want to come watch?"

I groaned. Asking me to get up this early was seriously inhumane. "I tired," I whined.

He kissed me on the nose. "I can call and cancel."

"No. Just go without me."

"I don't know," he murmured, brushing the hair off my cheek.

"I'll be fine. Adam's here."

"Are you sure?" I growled. He chuckled again. "I'll come back when I'm done."

"M'kay."

He kissed my cheek and tucked the blankets up around my chin. "I'll bring you a coffee."

Even after he was gone, the sheets still carried his scent. I breathed it in and slipped right back into a blissful sleep.

Unfortunately, my plan to sleep in and wallow in bed was short lived. Apparently Adam was a morning person like Cam (damn those early risers) and he started banging around in the kitchen, making me wonder what in the world he was doing.

With a groan, I rolled out of bed (I literally rolled out of bed and fell on my ass) and saw Cam's T-shirt lying on the floor. I picked it up and tugged it over my head, enjoying the way it smelled and felt against my skin. Then I grabbed a pair of yoga pants and put those on too.

I didn't bother combing my hair or brushing my teeth. Call it Adam's punishment for waking me up. I stumbled out of the bedroom and into the living, wiping the sleep from my eyes. Roxie's bedroom door opened and she came out looking as disgruntled as I, with a silk robe flapping behind her as she walked.

"What in God's name are you doing?" she grumped. "And what is that smell?"

"Your coffee maker is a piece of crap!" Adam yelled from the kitchen.

In guy speak, that meant he broke it, but he was blaming the poor appliance.

Roxie and I shared a glance and then went to survey the damage. I didn't know coffee makers could produce smoke. But ours was doing just that. It was also in the sink with water pouring over it from the faucet… which led me to believe that it had been on fire…

"I've actually never met anyone who couldn't use a coffee maker," I said, staring at the smoking, waterlogged appliance.

"Shit," Adam swore softly and ran a hand over the top of his head. "I'll buy you ladies another one."

Roxie giggled.

Adam looked at her sharply. "Are you laughing at me?"

She laughed harder. It made me laugh too.

Adam grinned. "Where the hell is Cam? And what's with all the chick food in the refrigerator?"

I sighed. "I bought guy food. Beer, bacon, eggs…"

"Yes, but those require actual cooking," Roxie said, stifling another giggle. "And it's clear that Adam knows nothing about cooking."

He wasn't amused.

"What do you usually eat, Adam?"

"I usually just hit a drive-thru," he muttered, and we both burst out laughing again. He scowled.

"Since I ruined the coffee maker, coffee's on me this morning. Even though you two hyenas don't deserve it, I'll even spring for donuts."

"I'll go with you," Roxie said, heading for her room where I assumed she was going to change out of her PJs.

"Well, that's a first," I said, watching her go.

"What?"

"I've yet to see her willingly leave the apartment this early in the morning."

Adam's chest puffed out. "I have a way with the ladies."

I snorted, hiding the fact that I secretly agreed with him.

"What do you want in your coffee?" he asked.

I shook my head. "You don't have to get me one. Cam's bringing one over for me after his surf lesson. But I won't argue with a donut."

He studied me a minute. "Want me to wait 'til Cam gets back before I go?"

I sighed. Everyone's concern was sweet, but I was an adult. I didn't need a babysitter. "No. I'm fine. Last night was scary, but I'm certainly not going to fall apart."

Roxie reappeared wearing a pair of cutoffs and a fitted tee. She had sunglasses already over her eyes. I laughed. "You better get the coffee. Looks like waking up this early isn't doing a body good."

Adam grabbed his keys off the counter and placed a hand on the small of Roxie's back as he led her to the door. "Lock this behind us," he called.

"Okay."

When the door closed, I let out a sigh. I loved my friends, but a few minutes alone seemed kind of appealing right now. I hadn't lied when I told Adam (or Cam) that I was okay. I was. But that didn't mean I didn't have some feelings to sort out in my mind for my own well-being.

I pushed away from the counter and spun, planning to go lock the door, but something on the counter caught my eye. It was the jar of rice that Cam had given me.

With everything going on, I had completely forgotten about my cell phone. Curious, I fished it out of the jar, snapped the battery into the back, and then hit the power button.

A few seconds went by and the screen flashed, coming to life. I smiled. It actually worked. Who'da thunk it?

I turned the phone over in my hands, making sure there weren't any scratches or damages, and then it made a series of small beeps. I flipped it back over to see that I had several voicemails.

All of them from my mother.

Crap. I had completely forgotten to call her back. She was probably worried to death. I glanced at the clock and noted that it was still a little early to call her so I went into my message box and played back the first voice message—the one that she left right before I dumped my phone in the melted ice.

I pressed the speaker button and my mother's voice filled the kitchen. *"Hi, honey, it's your mother. Seems we've been playing phone tag a lot lately. I hope everything is okay. I just wanted to let you know that John— the boy you went to high school with?"*

Yes, I remembered John well. He was the guy that told everyone I cheated with him, thus shooting down the whole tease rumor.

You're nothing but a little tease… The words from last night echoed in my head and I gasped.

My mother kept talking, although the room was beginning to tilt. *"John came by the house the other day. He hadn't realized you went away to college, and he thought he could speak with you. When I told him you weren't here, he asked me to pass along a message. He said he ran into Brody at a bar and he let your secret slip."*

Oh, this wasn't good. In fact, I was beginning to put together a puzzle I hadn't even realized I was assembling. As the pieces fit together, it revealed a very ugly picture.

"He seemed alarmed by this. He said Brody was upset. Honey, I don't understand—"

BEEP.

She had talked so long that the message cut her off. I was glad because I didn't want to hear any more. I ended the message and laid my phone on the counter, staring down at it.

The guy last night—the guy in the VIP room—wasn't a stranger. That's the reason he seemed familiar… because he was.

The scent of cologne suddenly washed over me and I gasped. Not only had half the guys in our school worn it when it came out, but so did Brody. I clearly remembered that fragrance from every date we ever had.

"I think you're getting the message a little late," said a voice from the kitchen entrance.

"Brody!" I gasped, spinning around. I guess I hadn't been imagining or just remembering the cologne. Brody was here, and he was wearing it now.

"So you recognize me now? Last night you seemed to have no clue. Or are all men just faceless objects for you to toy with?" He wasn't quite as tall as Cam, not reaching six feet, but he was broad through his upper body. He wore a pair of cargo shorts, a T-shirt, and a baseball cap. The hat may have shadowed his face, but it couldn't completely disguise the black eye, busted lip, and bruise across his cheekbone.

I now had no doubt it was him last night. Clearly, Cam's fists did a lot of damage.

"What are you doing here? How did you get in?"

"You know why I'm here," he said, his voice deadly calm. "You really should lock your doors."

"You need to leave."

He laughed and stepped farther into the kitchen.

I guess I suspected why he was here, but that didn't make it any easier to grasp. And even if my assumptions were right, I still had a hard time comprehending his behavior. In all the years I'd known Brody—*dated him*—I never thought he was capable of attacking me or coming into my home uninvited (with really bad intentions).

Yes, I'd kept the secret of the rumor I started, but in my opinion, he deserved it. He did it to me first (Hey, I was in high school. That's the kind of logic I was dealing with here). But even so… this was years ago. Who cared if John blurted out he really never had sex with me?

"Do you have any idea the amount of humiliation you caused me senior year?"

"I'm thinking it couldn't be any worse than walking through the hall and people whispering the words *ice* and *tease* at my back."

"What I said was the truth."

I cocked my head to the side. "Says who? You? Just because I wouldn't sleep with you back then gave you the right to spread rumors about me? You thought by labeling me a cock tease or some ice princess that you were going to make me finally give it up?"

"I was with you for years," he snapped. "Years of thinking it was going to happen and then just when I thought we were going to go all the way, you shut me down. And then you cheated on me. With the freaking quarterback. I was the laughing stock of the entire school. I became the guy who couldn't get it up. I became the guy that no girl wanted… Hell, some people even thought I was gay."

"You brought that on yourself."

His fists clenched and his eyes flashed. I realized I'd probably gone too far. He took another step toward me. I couldn't back away because my back was already pressed up against the counter.

"When you left for college, I thought people would forget, that no one would care anymore. But no one forgot. I was stuck in that fucking town where people made Viagra jokes and I could barely get a date. And then John came home from college for the summer. I saw him at the bar. He had one too many beers and started running his mouth. Imagine how I felt when he told everyone that he never slept with you. That you made it all up just to ruin my reputation."

"Brody, that was years ago. We were just kids."

"Yeah, but that lie followed me everywhere I went."

"I'm sorry," I murmured. I hadn't realized how badly the lie had hurt his reputation. I certainly hadn't meant to cause any long-lasting damage. Back then, I'd been a girl who just wanted the whispers to stop. I didn't want to be known as some frigid bitch.

I wasn't frigid… but I had acted like a bitch.

"We both lied and it got out of hand."

"Shut up!" he yelled. "You don't get to say you're sorry. There's only one thing that can make up for what you did."

Ice formed low in my belly. It was so cold that it spread through my veins, freezing everything in its path. "Go. Now. Or I'm calling the police." I reached around me and picked up my phone, getting ready to make good on my threat.

He lunged forward and snatched the phone out of my hand and threw it across the room, where it slammed against the wall and cracked, sliding down to the floor into several broken pieces.

"I'm not leaving until I get what I came here for."

"What's that?" I stuttered, very afraid I already knew.

His eyes raked over my body, making me feel sick and dirty all at once. "You're going to give me what was rightfully mine. I'm going to screw you and I'm going to make sure everyone knows that I did." He reached into his back pocket and pulled out a phone and held it up.

Oh my God, he was going to rape me and take pictures?

Like hell.

"I am *not* having sex with you," I said, my voice hard and clear.

"So you can dance for strangers? You can get naked and dance around on a table for them and let a sleazy bartender take shots out of your tits, but you won't give me something I earned?"

He was the stranger at the bar that night. He was watching Cam and me. It was him I felt staring at me from across the room.

"Sex isn't something you earn."

"I spent four years of my life putting up with you, thinking it would pay off, but all I got was a bad reputation and the quarterback stealing my thunder."

So what? I'd been some game to him? Some prize to be had? Did he plan on taking my panties and waving them around school after he'd claimed my virginity?

Sleazebag.

"I'm afraid you're too late," I spat. "My virginity has already been taken."

He let out a frustrated cry and leapt at me, trying to grab me. I shrieked and jumped back, reaching out and grabbing the jar full of rice. Without thinking twice, I swung it around and hit him across the face.

He stumbled backward, his hand going to his face. The glass of the jar was thick enough that it hadn't broken, so I held it out in front of me like a weapon.

Brody looked up, the left side of his face already swelling. "You're going to pay for that."

"You're the one that attacked my roommate, aren't you?"

He snarled. "Stupid bitch. I thought it was you. The minute she opened her mouth, I knew it wasn't."

Oh my God. Roxie had been attacked because of me. She lived in even more fear of her ex because of me.

"How did you find out where I lived?"

He looked smug. "You wrote it on a napkin at the bar. Lover boy was too busy to notice that I walked right up and took it."

I remembered that night. I had to give Cam my address again. Only he hadn't thrown away the napkin. It had been taken.

My stomach turned violently and I felt like I was going to be sick. I needed to get out of there.

I threw the jar at Brody's head and ran. I jolted past him as he knocked the jar away, and it landed on the floor, shattering. I could hear the uncooked grains of rice scatter across the linoleum, but I didn't stop. I rushed to the door and yanked on the handle.

It was locked. He locked it when he came in.

Frustrated, I reached for the lock, unlatching it and pulling open the door.

He caught me around the middle as I was rushing out outside. I screamed, but he covered my mouth with his hand and towed me backward, my feet dragging across the concrete as he went. I kept my eyes trained on the parking lot, praying to God someone would walk by and see what was happening.

Then he slammed the door shut.

His hand was still covering my mouth so I bit him. I bit down on the tender flesh of his palm so hard that I felt my teeth grind together. He gave a shout of pain and shoved me away. I skidded forward, tripping and sliding across the top of the coffee table, and then the whole thing tipped over and I landed on the ground.

The table landed on top of me and I struggled to get my bearings to push it away. But I didn't have to struggle long because Brody grabbed the table and flung it away. I heard some shattering and a crash, but I didn't look to see what it was because I was too terrified by the look on his face.

Something had snapped inside him. Something had truly gone haywire. He wasn't the same boy I remembered. He looked the same. His voice sounded pretty much the same… but his eyes… They didn't hold the spark they used to. They were flat and lifeless… almost like his conscience had completely vacated his body.

"Don't do this," I begged, surging to my feet and rushing around the back of the couch to put it between us.

"That little strip tease you did for me last night turned me on," he said, prowling closer. "You're still as hot as you used to be. Although, that purple stripe you had in your hair… It made you look like a slut. I'm glad it's gone."

Slowly I backed away, trying to gradually get to the door. Once I got there, I was going to run like hell.

"Take off your shirt."

"No."

"Is that his shirt? The bartender's? Is he the one you let have you? Tell me, Harlow, what's he got that I don't?"

My heart. Cam had my heart.

I wasn't about to tell him that, though. Something told me that would only make things worse. There was a half-empty water bottle on the side table beside the couch. I picked it up and chucked it at him. And then I threw the TV remote at him too. I know one of them connected because I heard his grunt. I raced to the door, but once again he caught me, this time when I was just shy of pulling it open.

He yanked me back against his body. He gyrated his front into my backside. He was hard. I started to cry silently. A knife appeared out of nowhere. He brandished it in front of my face while he whispered in my ear. "You're going to stop trying to get away. You're not going to scream. If you do, I will kill you when I'm done."

I'd rather die than be raped.

He grabbed me by the hair and swung me around, throwing me onto the floor. I started to get up, but he straddled me, pressing the knife to my throat. I froze and he smiled, shoving me back down.

There was a knock at the door. "Harlow, it's me."

I wanted to weep when I heard Cam's voice.

"Tell him to go away or I'll kill him," Brody whispered, scraping the knife over the surface of the delicate skin on my neck. I felt a warm rivulet of blood swell and then drip down my skin.

I drew in a deep breath. "Now isn't a good time, Cameron," I called.

"What's going on?" he asked, his voice concerned.

Brody jabbed the knife into my skin again and I whimpered. "I'm just not feeling well, Cameron," I yelled. "I'll call you later."

Please, God, let him realize the reason I called him by his full name—a name I never used—was because I was in desperate need of help.

"Okay, call me when you feel better. I'll come over."

"Sounds great," I said, trying to sound cheerful but failing miserably.

We both sat there for long moments, listening to the sound of his retreating footsteps. My heart fell. Fresh tears rushed down my cheeks. He didn't realize. He was leaving. My chance at getting out of this was gone.

Brody gave me a sick smile and pulled the knife away from my throat and used it to slice open Cam's T-shirt. Air brushed over my now naked, exposed chest. His rough hands grabbed me, squeezing.

I tried to buck him off and he laughed. "Oh yeah, baby, that's it. I like it when you wiggle beneath me."

I went stock still. I wasn't sure what to do.

He picked up his phone and I heard the little sound of the recorder coming on. "Tell everyone how good I feel," he instructed, training the camera on my bare chest as he reached out and twisted it roughly. I cried out.

There was a huge bang on the door and the wood cracked and splintered as it crashed in and hammered against the wall. Brody cursed and stood up, brandishing the knife once again.

"Watch out, Cam!" I cried, sitting up and scrambling away from Brody.

Cam's eyes glanced at me and widened. Then they narrowed and he looked back at Brody. "You sick son of a bitch…"

He lunged at him as Brody took a swipe at him with the knife. I cried out, but Cam dodged it, chopping down on his wrist and knocking the knife away. It clattered to the floor and Cam kicked it underneath the couch.

Brody swung, hitting Cam across the jaw, and his head snapped back. I got to my feet, looking for something else I could use as a weapon, and Cam and Brody went after each other like savages.

The sickening thuds of their fists would likely haunt my dreams for weeks. Cam delivered a series of blows right to Brody's face and blood spurted from his nose. Then Brody ducked low and ran at him, literally driving the top of his head into Cam's abdomen and bulldozing him into the wall.

"Cam!" I screamed and grabbed up the lamp on a nearby table. The cord ripped from the wall as I ran, and I brought it up, quickly swinging it down and hitting Brody solidly in the back of his head.

He crumpled to the floor, landing in a heap of arms and legs.

Cam bent down and looked at him. He was out cold so he felt around for a pulse.

Please, God, don't let him dead. I hadn't wanted to kill him. I just wanted him to stop.

"He's alive," Cam said, and a sob ripped from my throat.

Police sirens rang out in the distance.

Cam pulled the shirt over his head and pressed it to the cut on my neck. "What the hell did he do to you, baby?"

The gentle tone of his voice was my undoing and the dam broke, bringing forth a tidal wave of tears. He pulled me against his chest, holding me tightly to him and whispering words of love into my hair. "It's over now, sweetheart. He's not going to hurt you ever again."

I pulled back. "It's my ex-boyfriend from high school. I started a rumor about him years ago and he found out. He was here to—" My voice broke.

"Shhh, it's all right now. I know why he was here. He's lucky he's still alive."

Police cars screeched to a stop near the sidewalk and shouts rang from below. I could hear the officers pounding up the stairs, and then I heard Roxie and Adam screaming my name from across the parking lot.

I glanced back down at Brody, who was still unconscious on the floor. I felt guilty that he suffered over my lie. I felt guilty that I never thought about how he might feel. But still, breaking into my house, stealing my barrette, attacking Roxie, coming to the club, and then ultimately trying to rape me (and freaking recording it!) was not okay.

I prayed he got the help he needed and that he was locked away while he got it.

Cam looked down at me, his eyes searching my face. "I shouldn't have left here this morning."

"You're a lot earlier than I thought you would be."

"I cut the lesson short. I had this… bad feeling." He glanced at Brody. "Now I know why."

"I was afraid you didn't get my signal. I thought you left."

"I understood perfectly. You did good; you did real good."

The police stormed inside, taking in the damage and my bloodied, ripped clothes. They moved into action, cuffing Brody and studying the scene.

"Thank you for coming back," I told Cam, looking up to stare into his Hershey-colored eyes.

"I got you," he whispered, pulling me close once more. "And I'm not ever letting you go."

EPILOGUE

Four years later…

I pulled into the little parking lot and grinned at the sight of Cam's bike parked beside the white building. I rushed inside the surfboard shop only to find the space behind the counter empty, so I hurried through into the tiny office in the back. It was empty too.

"Cam?" I called out.

I pondered all the custom surfboards hanging on the wall as I waited for him to appear. He was so incredibly talented. Every board was unique and every one had a personality of its own.

I spun in a little circle, taking in the freshly painted walls and neatly organized display of wetsuits. He was finally living his dream. *Pura Vida Board Shop* was already a success, and I knew it would just keep on growing.

"Cam!" I called out again, impatient to feel his lips on mine.

When he still didn't respond, I gazed out the large front window and across the street toward the public access stretch of beach.

I grinned and raced out of the shop and across the pavement, tearing up the wooden steps and onto the walkway that led to the sand. The wind pulled at my shirt and I spotted him out in the water, sitting on his favorite surfboard, with a student beside him.

I rolled up my jeans, kicked off my flip-flops, and pushed my toes into the sun-heated sand. I felt his eyes the minute he saw me, and I lifted my hand and waved. He grinned and leaned into the guy who was with him, and I saw his mouth moving.

I watched as he expertly caught the next wave and rode it all the way in, jumping into the ankle-deep water beside me as his board washed up on shore.

"Hey," he said, hooking me around the waist and pulling me right up against his soaked chest.

I squealed and pressed myself closer. "You look good out there."

"You look good in my arms."

I giggled. "I went in the shop first. You need to hire someone to sit behind the counter."

He sighed and nuzzled my cheek with his nose. Wet strands of his hair clung to my skin and I wiggled around in his hold. "Replacing the girl who used to do it is impossible." He sighed.

Up until several days ago, I'd been the girl behind the counter of his shop. I loved working there, being by the beach all day, making out with my boss on my lunch break, and watching him make the most beautiful surfboards I'd ever seen.

Even though I loved it, I had my own dreams to follow.

"I start my new job on Monday," I said, excitement unfurling inside me.

He pulled back and grinned down at me. "Your office is going to be packed with a bunch of young college guys who just *can't* decide what to do with their lives," he said, pressing a hand to his chest and talking all dramatically.

I smacked him in his very toned stomach. "I doubt it."

He snorted. "You're the hottest career planner I've ever seen."

"Yeah?" I murmured, wrapping my arms around his neck. "Well, I'm taken."

He reached up and pulled my left hand down to look at the incredibly sparkly diamond gracing my finger. I still pinched myself whenever I looked at it. I was so unbelievably lucky to have someone like him.

"I can't wait to make you my wife," he said as he pressed a kiss to the ring he placed there just a few months before.

"Not much longer now." I sighed. We were going to have a wedding right here on the beach at sunset. I was going to wear white and no shoes, and Cam was going to wear a suit with an ocean-blue tie. In just two short weeks, I would be Mrs. Cameron Malone.

"Your job going to give you time off for our honeymoon?" he asked, his eyes straying to his student in the water.

"Of course. I didn't accept until they agreed."

His eyes came back to mine and he smiled. "Good. Now go sit your cute little ass over in the sand and quit distracting me from my job."

"Want me to go sit in the shop?"

He shook his head. "I want you right here with me."

Even after four years, his words still caused me to melt. I turned to go sit when he caught my hand and towed me back.

"Not so fast," he murmured, giving me a soft kiss. "I love you." He spoke right against my lips.

"I love you, too."

He kissed me again and then made a growling sound. "You. Me. Tonight." Then he wagged his eyebrows suggestively. His eyes softened and he kissed the tip of my nose. "Forever."

I couldn't think of anything better.

THE END

You lucky dog, you. Not only did you just read TEASE, but now you get a super exclusive sneak peak of TEMPT, the next *Take It Off* novel by Cambria Hebert!

Turn the page and enjoy!

Cambria Hebert

TEMPT

Sneak Peak

1

Scientists, philosophers, or whoever the group of people who sat around a desk and made up the list of the Seven Wonders of the World were wrong. There aren't seven. There are eight.

Number eight being men.

The reason men weren't added as a wonder of the world? Because men probably made up the list to begin with.

Even knowing trying to figure out a man, trying to have one in my life was a fruitless effort didn't stop me from having a relationship. It also didn't stop me from getting hurt.

Just when I was getting over that, my grandmother died.

So basically, I felt like I'd boxed about ten rounds, the entire time holding my own, and then I was knocked out. Cold.

And now here I was, wandering through the insanely large, insanely busy Miami International Airport so I could get on some plane and fly off to Puerto Rico because my grandmother's dying wish was for her ashes to be scattered over the ocean there—the place where she met my grandfather over fifty years ago.

How did I get elected for the job?

I was Grandmother's favorite. I was between jobs. I was down on my luck. I needed a free vacation to a beautiful place.

Right. Because flying to some foreign country (though, I guess technically, it's not a foreign country since it's considered a US territory) with a special suitcase just for the remains of my beloved grandmother and then parting with them to an ocean is considered some nice vacation.

Clearly, my family is a bunch of whackos.

Even still, I love my family and my heart still ached over my grandmother's passing, so here I was. The suitcase rolling along behind me tipped, and my bags toppled to the floor. With a great sigh, I stopped and turned, righting the one on wheels and then bending over to pick up the one I had balanced on top.

I slid it over and unzipped it, peering inside at the bubble-wrapped urn. Nothing appeared to be broken. "Sorry, Kiki," I murmured, using the name I called her since I could speak, and then zipped it closed. Deciding not to take any more chances with the smaller bag, I carried on, rolling the bigger one behind and carrying the other in my free hand. I also had a messenger-style purse strapped across my shoulder and it banged against my thigh with every step.

I made my way through the rapidly moving crowds, toward the gate I was told would have my ticket. Why I couldn't get an electronic one like everyone else in the modern age I would never understand.

As I approached the gate, I couldn't help but be distracted by a man leaning against one of the nearby walls. He was reading a newspaper, holding it up in front of his face so all I could see were the two long-fingered hands holding the paper and his body from the waist down.

He wore a pair of beat-up jeans, really beat up. Like, with holes and hanging strings. The denim was faded in some spots and the fabric seemed thin and likely soft to the touch. His T-shirt looked as well-worn as his jeans, except it didn't have any holes in it. All I could see of it was gray and just the front hem was tucked into his waistband, exposing a tan leather belt.

The way he leaned against the wall, kind of slouching with one foot out farther than the other, drew attention to his shoes. The boots were the same color as his belt and they appeared sturdy and not nearly as used as his clothes.

I couldn't tell you why I was so drawn to him. That was all I could see. He just looked like some regular (albeit lazy) guy waiting around for his plane to arrive. Although, he was reading the *New York Times,* which made me snort. He didn't really look like the kind of guy that would stand around reading that paper.

I snorted to myself again. He probably had a *Penthouse* just inside the paper and was really reading that.

My gate was off to my right and I turned, eyeing the counter and noting that there weren't as many people in this section of the airport as the other parts I'd just walked through. The woman behind the counter had perfectly combed hair slicked up into a bun on the back of her head. She was dressed in a navy blazer with the airline's name on the breast, and she sported a polite look on her face. When I stopped at the counter, I parked my bags next to me and flipped the top of my messenger bag open to reach inside for my wallet and ID.

"My name is Ava Malone. I was told my ticket to Puerto Rico would be here waiting for me."

The woman took my ID and looked at it and then handed it back to me. Her manicured fingers flew over the keyboard behind the counter and then she paused and looked up. "You're plane is already here."

Alarm spiked through me. "Am I late? I thought I was an hour early. As soon as I get my ticket, I'll go board. Will they hold the plane for me?"

She gave me an odd sort of look. "I'm sure it will wait, seeing as how you are the only passenger."

Confusion made me speechless. I felt my face scrunch up in an odd sort of way as her words replayed through my head. "I don't understand," I said slowly. "I can't be the only person flying to Puerto Rico today."

She shook her head. "Definitely not. But you are the only one who had a private plane come and fetch her."

A private plane? To fetch me?

"You must have the wrong person," I said, holding up my ID again. "You should check again. I should just have a ticket here. For one of the commercial flights."

"You're Ava Malone, correct?"

I glanced at my ID just to be sure. That's what it said, right there beside my horribly embarrassing photo. "Appears that's me," I muttered.

She smiled. "Your pilot is around here somewhere," she said, craning her neck to look around. Her eyes settled on someone across the room and she smiled. "He's right over there."

I turned, following her gaze. There next to the guy with ratty jeans was an older gentleman in a suit, holding a briefcase. I lifted my hand to wave at him. He got this puzzled look on his face and then waved uncertainly.

"Are you sure?" I said, feeling my cheeks heat with embarrassment as I glanced back at the woman.

I turned back around to glance again. The gentleman with the suit was gone. My eyes darted around, looking for him, but once again were drawn to the guy with the newspaper. He must have felt my stare because his head shot up and I saw his eyes peek over the top.

Slowly, the newspaper came down and something else was lifted. A giant white index card.

It had my name on it.

My stomach did a summersault and my heart started thumping erratically.

Why would that ratty jean wearing, *Penthouse* reading guy have a sign with my name on it?

"See," the woman said from behind. "That's him. He has a sign with your name on it."

"*That's* my pilot?"

The woman at the counter giggled. She actually giggled like a schoolgirl.

Shoot. Me. Now.

I gathered up my bags and took a few steps forward, intent on finding out just what the hell was going on, when he lowered the oversized card.

My steps faltered.

The suitcase trailing along behind me kept going and rammed into my calves, making me stumble, and I pitched forward with a startled cry, knowing I was going to go down and praying to the heavens that I didn't crush Kiki when I fell.

The last thing I saw was the stupid *New York Times* paper fluttering to the floor as Kiki and I plunged disastrously toward the floor. But then he was there, grabbing up the suitcase, saving it from my clumsiness.

I, however, was not so lucky.

I fell.

Hard. In fact, if my arms hadn't been free, I would have fallen directly on my face. Thankfully, my hands slapped against the hard floor, saving my nose from being rearranged. When I hit, I fell over, rolling onto my back, and lifted my hands, staring at them in front of my face. My palms stung from the fall and I cringed imaging how many germs were now crawling all over them from touching the nasty airport floor.

"Are you okay?" said a voice above me.

I jerked my arms down, propping myself up on my elbows, and lifted my eyes.

I remembered why I fell all over again.

Light-green eyes speared me from within a face that, even if he left right now and I never ever saw him again, I would not forget. His face was so striking that it would be etched into my mind forever.

His eyes were the color of green sea glass. A bright green but light because it had spent time tumbling around the ocean floor. They were a striking contrast against the rest of him. He was all dark and bronze with a head full of thick dark hair that curled around on his head. It was messy like he never combed it—though I would think that combing curls would only give him an Afro.

His skin was olive toned, bronzed like he never left the sun, and he had sharp features—a straight nose, full lips, and cheekbones that sat high just beneath those eyes, which were lined in impossibly thick, impossibly dark lashes.

He was tall (or maybe he just looked that way because I was sprawled on the floor) and had a lean build, but he looked strong—the kind of strength that came naturally, not the kind of bulk that came from the gym.

As I stared at him like a complete idiot, he set down the suitcase carefully and squatted beside me. My breath caught (or maybe I just forgot I needed to breathe) when he got closer. He was freaking beautiful. Yeah, I know, guys aren't supposed to be beautiful, but he was. There was no other word that I could think of that would describe him better.

I was still staring as he reached out and grasped me by the shoulders. The heat of his hands radiated through my T-shirt and practically zapped me back to reality. "Did you hurt yourself?"

Oh my God, he had an accent.

As if perfection just upped its game and got even better.

It wasn't a full-on accent. It was a barely there—a slight roll of the tongue that caused chills to rise up across my scalp and race over my head and down my spine.

I nodded because speaking was still not an option.

"You're Ava Malone?"

Say it again. Something inside me begged. *Please just say my name one more time.*

The desperation going on inside my own head was what fully shocked me out of my trance. There was no way I was about to succumb to some beautiful disaster of a man. And yes, I did know that he was a complete disaster because there was no way on this planet that a man who looked like him could be anything but trouble.

"Yes, that's me. I'm fine," I said, shaking off his hands and standing up. "Nice catch by the way." I gestured to the suitcase that contained Kiki.

He grinned. His teeth were blindingly white against his tanned skin. "Sorry, it had to be one or the other."

He didn't look sorry, the snake. He probably enjoyed watching me bust my butt. "Uh-huh," I said, reaching for the suitcase with the urn.

He reached out and took it first.

My back teeth clenched together.

"I can get my bags."

"After what I just saw, I think your grandmother would be safer in my arms."

That should have insulted me. It should have alarmed me that he knew what was inside. Instead, all I got was a vision of being tucked against his chest, with bronzed, strong arms wrapped around me and the beating of his heart beneath my ear.

I needed a drink.

A stiff one.

I pushed my raging thirst and apparent horniness to the back of my mind to say, "How did you know what was in there?"

"Was it a secret?" he asked, a little smile playing on his lips.

"Are you a psychic?"

He laughed. It was a warm, rich sound that reminded me of brewing coffee on a cold, early morning. "No. I'm not psychic. I'm just your ride."

"My ride?" I won't even describe the vision that floated through my mind when he said *that*.

He nodded like I was two. "Yes. Me, pilot. You, passenger." He pointed between us while he spoke.

"You're a pilot?"

He fished a pilot's license out of the back of his pocket and held it up. "That's what it says."

I scoffed. "I'm surprised that didn't fall out of the pocket of those holey pants."

His smile spread across his face like a slow, contagious disease. A disease that people would actually line up to catch. "My jeans hold in everything that's important."

I blushed.

Like, seriously.

To cover up my juvenile behavior, I squinted at the name on the license he was still holding up. "Nash Prescott," I read.

"At your service."

"You don't look old enough to be a pilot."

"You don't look old enough to travel alone."

I rolled my eyes.

"I'm twenty-three. I've been flying since I was a teenager. I've got more flight hours than you have hair on your head."

"Doubtful." I had really thick, long blond hair.

He cocked his head to the side and studied me. "Anyone ever tell you that you look like Kate Hudson?"

The actress? Daughter of Goldie Hawn. Actually, yes, they had. "Nope."

He smiled like he knew I was lying.

There was no way I was getting on a plane with him. "I'm sorry you had to come here all the way from… well, from wherever you came."

"Puerto Rico," he said, and when he did, his accent came out full force. It made the place sound exotic and enticing. "I flew here from Puerto Rico."

"You flew here to pick me up?"

He nodded.

"But why?"

"Our abuela's were great friends." He explained. "When your family called to arrange for her ashes to be scattered, my abuela offered for me to come and pick you up."

"So they volunteered you to come here like my family volunteered me to go there."

He smiled. "I guess both our families are loco." He used his pointer finger to draw circles around the side of his head.

I giggled. Then I sighed. "Look, I'm sorry you had to come here. I'll just go to the ticket counter and get a commercial flight and let you get back to your… whatever it is that you do."

"Right now my job is to take you to Puerto Rico, where you will stay with my grandmother and then be escorted to the place where you are to spread these ashes." He gestured toward the case in his hand.

"I'm supposed to stay with you?" I asked, feeling my eyes bug out of my head.

"Not me. My abuela."

"Abuela? That's Spanish for grandmother, right?"

He nodded.

"You don't live with her?"

He chuckled softly. "I think that would cramp my style."

Exactly. And why was I still here talking to him? I started to walk away. He stopped me. His hand was like a rope wrapping around my wrist. It was like a handcuff trapping me to a jail cell, a vise around my heart.

"*Esperate*," he said softly. The word literally rolled right off his tongue.

I turned back. You would've too.

My eyes locked on his, searching their translucent depths. "I really hope you didn't just insult me." Even if he did, I really didn't care. It was the sexiest insult I'd ever heard.

His smile was lopsided. I thought I might faint. "I said wait a second."

I glanced at his hand wrapped around my wrist, then back up. He saw me looking. He didn't let go. "There's no need for another ticket when I can take you."

I hesitated. What excuse could I give? I couldn't exactly say, "I'm sorry, but you are way too sexy for me to have to sit alone with on a plane for any amount of time." It wasn't like he drove a couple hours to pick me up. He freaking flew a plane to get me. He was doing it as a favor for his grandmother.

"How do I know you aren't really a kidnapper?"

"Two reasons," he said, releasing my arm.

I lifted an eyebrow.

"One," he said, holding up a finger. "I don't have to kidnap women. If I want one, I get one."

I actually believed that. He probably had women lined up at home.

"And two," he said, flicking up a second finger. "My abuela is Marisol Castillo."

Again, his accent was more pronounced when he spoke her name. A name that I recognized. She was indeed my grandmother's very dear friend.

"Your abuela is Marisol?"

He produced a picture from the same pocket where he kept his ID and held it out. It was of my grandmother, Cora, and Marisol. I had seen this same image hanging on her refrigerator practically all my life.

I took the photo out of his hands, staring down at Kiki with tears blurring my vision. I missed her. I missed her so much. "Okay," I said softly. "I'll go with you."

He reached around me with his free hand and took my rolling suitcase. "Let's go."

I trailed along behind him like a puppy, mentally telling myself I was going to regret this.

Ready for more of Nash and Ava's story?
Purchase and read **TEMPT** October 2013!

ACKNOWLEDGEMENTS

Writing a novel about a stripper was fun… lol. It was also a little hard because I've never been a stripper (everyone on Earth is sighing with relief). Although, a little fun fact for you: when I was young, someone offered me five hundred bucks to strip at a bachelor party (plus tips!). I said no. I can't imagine what being a stripper must be like. So, if Harlow's experience at stripping seems a little unreal, that's because I was writing her the way I think stripping would be and maybe if I had to be a stripper, the way I would approach it.

LOL.

I have been to Myrtle Beach many times, and Broadway at the Beach is one of my favorite places there. The Ripley Aquarium is a really great place to explore.

I want to acknowledge Cassie McCown, my wonderful and super-talented editor, for always working the bugs out of all my books. To Regina Wamba, who did the original photography for the cover (as soon as I saw this image, I had to have it for Harlow), and then she took the photograph and turned it into the cover. Another fun fact for you: Harlow orignally had blond hair. Then I saw this picture and I changed Harlow's hair dark to match the cover.

Without Cassie and Regina, my books wouldn't look and read as good as they do. They are my own little go-to team that I couldn't imagine working without. Thank you, ladies. You rock!

To my writing buddies, Amber and Cameo, you know I love you and thank you for always being there. For all the girls in Indie Inked, I love you all too, and it's so great to have a great group of authors that can talk to each other and support one another. I so appreciate it.

To author Tara Brown, thanks so much for always being around to chat, for inspiring me to amp up my writing (to the new adult level), and for always encouraging me. Thanks for the introductions and all the enthusiasm you always show when I tell you about my latest project. You really inspire me with your success and your down-to-earth approach. You rock, too!

To my husband Shawn and Sergeant Major Marc Braswell (of the United States Marine Corps) for constantly teasing me about needing to write a book called *Shades of a Latte Stripper*. You two didn't think I would actually do it, did you? Well, here ya go… Here's your book about a stripper. Pardon me for changing the title, but I think mine is better.

This was a really fun book to write, probably one of the most fun I have written so far, and I really hope you all enjoy reading it.

Thank you all so much for all the emails, messages, and support you give me on a daily basis. It's because of you that I continue to write!

Cambria Hebert

Cambria Hebert is the author of the young adult paranormal *Heven and Hell* series, the new adult *Death Escorts* series, and the new adult *Take it Off* series. She loves a caramel latte, hates math, and is afraid of chickens (yes, chickens). She went to college for a bachelor's degree, couldn't pick a major, and ended up with a degree in cosmetology. So rest assured her characters will always have good hair. She currently lives in North Carolina with her husband and children (both human and furry), where she is plotting her next book. You can find out more about Cambria and her work by visiting http://www.cambriahebert.com.

Facebook: https://www.facebook.com/pages/Cambria-Hebert/128278117253138
Twitter: https://twitter.com/cambriahebert
Pinterest: https://pinterest.com/cambriahebert/pins/
GoodReads:
http://www.goodreads.com/author/show/5298677.Cambria_Hebert

ALSO CHECK OUT THESE EXTRAORDINARY AUTHORS & BOOKS:

Alivia Anders ~ Illumine
Cambria Hebert ~ Death Escorts Series (*Recalled* & *Charmed*)
Angela Orlowski Peart ~ Forged by Greed
Julia Crane ~ Freak of Nature
J.A. Huss ~ Tragic
Cameo Renae ~ Hidden Wings
A.J. Bennett ~ Now or Never
Tabatha Vargo ~ Playing Patience
Tiffany King ~ Meant to Be
Beth Balmanno ~ Set in Stone
Lizzy Ford ~ Zoey Rogue
Ella James ~ Selling Scarlett
Tara West ~ Visions of the Witch
Heidi McLaughlin ~ Forever Your Girl
Melissa Andrea ~ The Edge of Darkness
Komal Kant ~ Falling for Hadie
Melissa Pearl ~ Golden Blood
Alexia Purdy ~ Breathe Me
L.P. Dover ~ Love's Second Chance
Sarah M. Ross ~ Inhale, Exhale
Brina Courtney ~ Reveal
Amber Garza ~ Star Struck
Anna Cruise ~ Maverick

Cambria Hebert